41/6

A CLASSIC DEATH

By Amy Marsland

A CLASSIC DEATH
CACHE-CACHE

A CLASSIC DEATH

AMY MARSLAND

PUBLISHED FOR THE CRIME CLUB BY

DOUBLEDAY & COMPANY, INC.

GARDEN CITY, NEW YORK

1985

All of the characters in this book
are fictitious, and any resemblance
to actual persons, living or dead,
is purely coincidental.

Library of Congress Cataloging in Publication Data

Marsland, Amy Louise.
A classic death.

I. Title.
PS3563.A7226C6   1985   813'.54
ISBN 0-385-19997-X

Library of Congress Catalog Card Number 84-28711
Copyright © 1985 by Amy Marsland
All Rights Reserved
Printed in the United States of America

First Edition

Dedicated to
BILL
With thanks to Gerry Raine,
Ruth Tuttle, and Jack Deuel

A CLASSIC DEATH

CHAPTER 1

The holiday quartet lay in the curve of the sand, faces outward toward an immense and luminous sky, a sea constantly whispering to itself in the sweep of an endless swell. For animation, in the manner of the pointillists of the eighties, a foreground flecked with scarlet, orange, blue—which, if you squinted, resolved itself into minuscule bikinis, their tawny wearers fading into the fawn of the beach. Strange polyps stranded by the tide, striped umbrellas thrust out their tangled limbs. Brown children, blue-tighted, squabbled at the water's edge; a youth ran past, curly and brown as an Italian, silver cross bouncing upon his hairy pectorals . . . "Why don't you wear a cross?" Laura demanded suddenly of François.

He, while the other three lay, sat characteristically upright, attention upon the horizon; and snorted, "Because, *voilà,* I am not an *abbé.*"

"Tiens!" said Marie-Gisèle ironically; she was applying tanning lotion. Laura, fairer of skin and prudent, had put hers on already, in the hotel room. Marc, between them, lay facedown on the blanket, unmoving. "That is an answer? She wants you to wear one, your lovely Laura; she thinks it is sexy," and the last word, in English, emerged from Marc's muffled lips in comical precision. François snorted again, and, rising on her elbows, Laura pursued her curiosity. "Yes, but why not? Is it a sort of class thing, like pierced ears in America?"

"Is *that* a class thing?" Marie-Gisèle was surprised. "Oh, yes—or it used to be. Little Italian girls and other such foreigners—no proper Anglo-Saxon would . . . 'Think of the risk of infection!' " And she mimicked horrified accents.

"Imagine—and now you find nothing charming in earrings except for pierced ears!"

"Oh, us too, I suppose, now. I speak from my childhood: odd to think Franchot's childhood will not be the least like it!"

"Oh but"—Marie was practical—"nobody's childhood is what it was thirty years ago; our children live in a new world, isn't it—computers and satellites and games of the video—none of us will know what to tell them."

"I will," said Marc, his muffle growling.

"Ah you, policier!"

"But still"—Laura was stubborn—"I would like to know if Franchot can wear a cross when he is older, and if not, why not?"

"Think of Solange then!" François was categorical. "Imagine her face, that freethinker, when you present her a grandson with a cross on a silver chain round his neck: is that good enough for you?"

As an image, it was good enough; it was not an explanation, but it was good enough. Laura had had adequate opportunity to observe that, for all their vaunted logic, the French were no better than members of more irrational nations at explaining their taken-for-granted idiosyncrasies. Of course, it was possible to unearth the context of crosses: if you started with Clovis, added the Wars of Religion (fought not far from here), stirred in Henry IV's "Paris is well worth a mass," the Revolution's Goddess of Liberty, and the Vendée (fought not very far from here either), and swirled on a final frosting, the anticlerical nineteenth century; but it would scarcely be worth one second of holiday time. Still—"Do you wear a cross?" she asked Marc, suddenly.

"Of course not!" said Marc incontrovertibly. "I am a policeman."

They all laughed; Marc rolled sidewise, gave Marie-Gisèle

a push, and subsided again onto his stomach. "You know—this was a good idea."

Soft grunts, sighing subsidences, agreed that it was. It had come up, idly, on a rainy February Sunday afternoon: the Taverniers were having dinner with the LeBretons and, elbows angled under chin over the last of the wine, Marie-Gisèle had said, "Are you going on holiday this summer? Marc has put in for late August."

François admitted that he expected late August too. It was true that was the time when, every other Parisian on holiday, Paris deserted was as sweet to sip as dessert wine *chambré*—but it was also when his clients were absent and therefore undemanding. And of clients he had many, since his marriage to Laura ("that American who rescued Monnet") and his own involvement in the affair which saw France's grand old man held to atomic ransom and Laura's husband, the subversive brain behind the kidnapping, dead at François's own hands. The contacts, the friends he had made then, were some of them highly placed, and if the LeBretons were not yet of "le monde" they were most assuredly of the world as it pertained to the legal profession. Marc, whose inspectorship in the Police Judiciaire had come as a result of the same affair, was certainly not of "le monde" at all: but his old friendship with François had remained unchanged, and the two couples saw one another at least monthly.

"Si on y allait ensemble!" Marie-Gisèle's inspiration was sudden; if she had thought about it she would not have spoken, not yet confident enough of herself to take liberties with the LeBretons' freedom of action. But François raised an interested eyebrow, and Laura's astonishment had pleasure in it.

"Oui—mais où, 'y?'" inquired Marc, critical. "All the good places, you know, must be taken far in advance for August—if we do want to go together we will have to plan soon!" There ensued a gabble, lengthy, inconclusive, and delightful: there is nothing more enjoyable, on a rainy February Sunday, than discussing the comparative merits and demerits of places

where the sun shines. The Riviera, Marc proposed, though with some hesitation out of respect for his salary; Laura said, "Hot and crowded. Northern Spain?" "Hot and crowded and full of Germans," said François, who was not a Bocheophile. "What about the Jura, or Lake Genève?" "Lovely scenery—all vertical," was Marie-Gisèle's comment, "though if we take the children . . ."

Around this topic there was a considerable detour. A one-year-old baby and two active boys aged respectively eight and nine are not ideal holiday companions. But the French, unlike the English, do not automatically feel children under the age of reason should be seen as infrequently as possible and heard not at all. Maternal guilt in Marie-Gisèle and Laura crippled their normal desire to say, "A holiday ought to be a holiday, *quoi!*" and it took Marc eventually to say it for them. *"Les vacances sont les vacances, quoi!* If taking them to the Luxembourg on Sundays is not enough . . . and when do I see my wife alone except on holiday?"

"Before six and after ten," said Marie-Gisèle smartly, "and half the time too tired to make use of it. If I had known what a promotion meant . . ." she rolled her eyes skyward.

"Only take me to Normandy or Brittany," Marc promised, "and you will see—ah!"

"Very well—as long as it's not Alsace!" and at this reference to Marc's old boss, the Alsatian Steinhauser, they all laughed. "It would be pleasant to swim," observed François, "but what does one do in Brittany in the evening?—aside from *that,* I mean?"

So in the end Marc said, *"Voyons*—we will take out the map of France and Marie will close her eyes and place a magic finger on it. Wherever she chooses—we go—and if we know it, so much the better. If not, we explore—agreed?"

"The French," said Marie-Gisèle severely, "do not explore; they pick one superior place and go there every summer." Nevertheless she closed her eyes, stood, jabbed, and cried, "There!" triumphantly.

Everyone looked; she had picked the emptiest place in the

whole of France, the Atlantic Coast between La Rochelle and Bordeaux. *"Tiens!* I have never been there." François. "Nor I." "Nor I." "Nor I."

So here they were, in August, at Pontaillac-Royan. It had taken a good deal of interim planning. Solange and Robert had agreed instantly to take Franchot, "diapers and all" said Solange, "and he has visited often enough so he will not feel strange here." The Tavernier grandparents, however, came in two families, and Marie-Gisèle spent a great deal of time wondering, "Which? Where first? Will it give offense if . . ." and, most agitating of all, "Do they mean what they say, Laura? Can they really want those two demons for a week each?" "You must take them at their word, I think; I presume they are old enough to speak comprehensibly?"

Accommodations then had to be organized—in the end Laura went, leaving Franchot for the day with Marie-Gisèle, and returned pleased but dubious. "I have double rooms for each of us, with shared bath—it is very haute bourgeoise, Marie, and fairly expensive. But it has a lovely view and garden—it used to be a Bordeaux wine merchant's villa—and they serve meals which smelled to me very good. Hotels are so vast, and pensions really not quite so comfortable as we may want—but if you think you won't like it, I shall write to cancel today!"

Marie-Gisèle thought they would like it. *"Un peu d'élégance, quoi!* But are there things to do and see, besides swimming?"

"Oh yes—when we are sunburned we can drive inland and study Romanesque churches on the pilgrim route to Compostela!"

In fact, Laura had harbored a doubt or two about spending their holiday as a foursome. Marc was all right—men were always all right if they didn't fuss—but in the nature of things it meant spending a good deal of time in Marie-Gisèle's company; and in two years she had not really come to know Marie-Gisèle that well. She was—or appeared—open, frank, and full of zest; in the months of Laura's pregnancy, she had been cheerful, expert, and supportive; and if Franchot cried too long in the night Marie was the first person she would call. But since Marc's promotion she had shown a tendency to *arrivisme*. There was this question of the name, for instance. Marie's family in Normandy were prosperous but unassuming peasants, and all her life she had been called Marie—but a year ago she had decided to adopt her second name and become not plain Marie but the more elegant Marie-Gisèle. She would have liked, she confided to Laura, to change to Gisèle *tout court*, but Marc flatly refused to abandon Marie; now if Laura made a point of calling her Marie-Gisèle?

Laura tried conscientiously to remember the double name, and she understood in a way, but—would Marie like Romanesque churches? would Gisèle? Or, worst of all, would she "like" them in the wrong way? . . . Well, of course, just because husbands were intimate there was no reason for wives to be: and what was intimacy, in any case? François and Marc, she was sure, did not discuss their wives, their clothes, their dreams as close women friends did; true intimacy, she supposed, was more a matter of character and . . . trust; the confidence that whatever the emergency the other would respond instantly, without question. And at least where Franchot was concerned did she not already have that with Marie?

Now Marie-Gisèle stretched like a cat and grinned. "Oh, that was a good dinner we had last night! And the company at the villa is interesting, don't you think?" "Mm." Laura had not paid much attention to them, too intent on admiring the cream-painted paneled dining room with its pots of geraniums and cactus and cool fern; the Villa Brise de Mer had on its three floors perhaps a dozen rooms, and not all the inhabitants had turned out to dine. A professor and his radiantly white-haired wife, though professor of what she did not yet know; an older man with a much younger female companion; a large dual family from Turin who had the whole top floor; a husband and wife and their son, the sandy-haired husband in espadrilles rather too patronizing to his young son and the mother overattentive. But Marie knew everything; or everything at any rate that could be garnered in a day. "That man with the little boy, he's a journalist, madame told me—not in Paris however, I think Marseille. But the other couple, the older man with the young wife—that's Jean Calvet."

"And who," inquired Marc, taking the words from Laura's mouth, "is Jean Calvet?"

"An industrialist," François was not quite ironic, "who wants to become a Minister. Take note, Marc; he may even hope to become Minister of Justice!"

"And will he?" Laura was curious.

"*Ça depend.* Not under Mitterand of course—he belongs with all the other industrialists to the RPR. But with labor, peasants, and truckers against him, just how long will Mitterand last? And Calvet has been particularly effective both in the Députés and the country at large in putting succinctly just why socialism is counterproductive . . . I believe he has also dug out some particularly embarrassing instances *where* it is so, too. So you see if the left goes down at the next election, his ambition may prove quite realistic."

"But what is he doing, then, in our pension? It is extremely comfortable and quiet, but I would have expected . . . oh, Deauville and the Ritz!"

"His district is just north of here; he is mending fences, and it does not do, you know, to overawe your constituents." But François's attention was down by the shore where a troupe of children, the journalist's son among them, were digging in the sand; and, "Next year we shall take Franchot to the sea," Laura resolved.

"*Ah, le voilà, justement!* And the *allumeuse!*" Marie-Gisèle flicked her lashes to where, at the edge of the sea, Jean Calvet emerged, top hair thinning, tough muscles beaded with brine, energy and power in the speed with which he plowed through the waves to the sand. She, his wife in her perfect figure and her white bathing suit rose, put a delicate hand on his hairy arm in a gesture which implied both possession and being proudly possessed by. "But why do you call her an *allumeuse?*" Laura inquired over Marc's recumbent head.

"Watch her. Every inch of her body says 'Watch me!' but also, 'If you touch I'll chop off your fingers.' Tch!"

"Your fingers! Nothing more?" Even buried in the blanket Marc's irony was perceptible. Laura looked. Mme. Calvet's dark hair, undulant and deep as a night forest, drowned the tiny face and its exquisite features: the coral bud of a mouth, the eyes which had seen most of the world and were not impressed . . . From the sculptured curve of the shoulder to the smooth arch of the instep her skin glowed a delicate amber; and one knew without need of evidence that she tanned nude, no white demarcations to mar the composition . . . A smouldering flame which could never itself be burned. The pair turned toward the walk and the villa; and François, eyes still at the sea's edge, exclaimed. "But what is he doing, *cet enfant-là?*"

At the rim of the smooth crescent of beach embraced by low headlands, the journalist's small son had found a rock and was trying, by main force, to cleave it with the edge of his sand shovel. Thwack, thwack, the blue blade flew up and down with demonic energy; Laura cried out, Marie-Gisèle exclaimed, and in the same instant the inevitable happened; the shovel leaped from its handle, the blade struck the boy square in the center of his forehead, and the white sand ran abruptly red while the child stared at it astonished.

Laura and Marie-Gisèle, competitive one might have said in some impromptu mothers' race, sprinted together; they arrived just as he was starting to cry and his mother, a hundred feet away, to rise from her beach towel. In a moment, however, she was upon them, then, as if the two other women created a defensive wall, rebounded in shock. "But what has he, Jacquot, *mon pauvre Jacquot!*" She stared and wrung her hands in horror.

Concealing their instant scorn, Laura and Marie-Gisèle each took a hand, murmuring consolations as they led the roaring Jacquot toward the beach walk. "But *mon Dieu,* the

blood, is he dying? Do something!" She ran backward in front
of them. "Scalp wounds bleed a great deal," said Marie-Gisèle repressively, *"ce n'est pas grave, probablement."* Laura,
thinking he might all the same need a stitch or two, searched
about her—where does one keep a handkerchief in a bathing
dress? but Marie-Gisèle of course had a clutch of Kleenex in
her bag. Holding the wad awkwardly to his head, hampered
at every step by the mother's darts and dashes, she stopped at
the low beach steps and said firmly, "Go call the doctor."
"But who—which?"

And so it was, that they beheld for the first and only time
the Madwoman of Pontaillac. Astonishing vision, as she
paraded above—even Jacquot stopped crying, mouth open.
Her skirts, long, frothy in a garden party style of sixty years
ago, swished as she strolled; the flowered fabric, its collar
high-ruffled in the fashion of yesteryear, was threadbare beneath the tight waist, and the flounce of the hem had, here
and there, vanished away. Her white gloves, however, were
spotless, and her parasol, true silk in an elegant shade of rose,
was tasseled at the crook. A hat, of some aged straw sprouting
in ribbon and flowers, doubled the sheltering shade on her
face with its crinkled remnants of beauty; a small girl behind
her, ice halfway to her mouth, in maillot so skimpy it would
have horrified her grandmother as much as this grandmoth-
erly costume astonished her, stood stunned at the spectacle.
But, oblivious to this audience, she sailed past, gave her parasol a single twirl, closed it, and crossed the road to speak to
the flower seller at his cart by the villa's curving pilastered
garden fence.

"Well!" said Marie-Gisèle, beyond words, and Jacquot, reminded, started to cry again. "Come, we will ask madame,
she will find a doctor who will tell us if we need a stitch or two
to preserve your beauty, *hein?*"

Looking both ways, they started to cross the road, but at
the villa gate a traffic jam had developed. Two young men,
lithe and dark, had come up the walk just as the professor and
his wife were emerging; behind them the Calvets and the

emergency party, stalled, thronged the gateway. Seeking a shortcut, Laura glimpsed the old woman; ten feet away, she was staring at the crowd, on her face an expression of pure astonishment. Her mouth opened as if to speak; one hand flew out, then back to her breast, and she staggered . . . Oh no! thought Laura, not a second emergency! the doctor . . . But the flower vendor, anxious, moved forward to help her to a promenade bench, the path cleared abruptly, and Marie-Gisèle tugged Jacquot, screams now earsplitting at the thought of stitches, toward the villa. Madame, blond pompadour as dignified as her establishment, was already at the steps waiting. "Ah, a little accident! We will telephone Dr. Trebuchet immediately, he will soon take care of it!" And, to Marie-Gisèle in lower tones, "If you will take him through to the kitchen, madame—blood, you know, is so difficult to remove from the carpets!"

CHAPTER 2

Abandoned by their women, the first thing men do is to go have a drink; it is a primitive instinct, like that of the elk for the waterhole. François and Marc were no exception; Marc stood, looking after them, and picked up the blanket. François rescued Laura's beach bag, and they adjourned to the shade of the humble but rather pleasant estaminet which, just above the beach on the headland, offered shade and a splendid view of the sea. They did not, however, look at it; they stood at the bar and ordered two white wines. "Fifteen minutes of sun they tell me," Marc observed cheerfully, "is enough for the first day." But François was meditative. "Tell me—do children always take so much of their mothers' attention?"

"Yes," said Marc, looking into his glass. "The only difference is that, as they grow up, they get noisier about it."

Pas possible! You," said François grimly, "are a false friend. Do you remember, the day before I got married, you told me I would never regret it, that my life stretched before me now serene and contented?"

"I spoke," said Marc virtuously, "of marriage only. *Families* were not included in my prediction."

The large man lifting a beer at François's elbow was amused. "Do I gather," he inquired, "that you are speaking to a recent father?"

"You do. And are you yourself a man of experience?"

"Vast. I have seven offspring, though four of them are now married and on their own here and there. And I agree that fatherhood is a heavy burden; but a man is required to bear it cheerfully, it is his gravest obligation to posterity."

François eyed him with interest; he was by no means as gregarious as Marc, but the cheerful solemnity with which the judgment was proffered intrigued him. Franchot, no doubt about it, was the joy of his life; he woke sometimes at four in the morning to say to himself astounded, "I have a son!" But the practical mechanics of the thing eluded him; babies were so delicate, so unfathomable; what did they think, for instance? Yet the obligation was undoubtedly there: however ignorant, one must bring them up properly. "That is true, that is very true," he observed judiciously.

"But as for taking their mothers' attention, there is a solution for that, and if you wish I will offer it to you—we old fathers, after all, have a duty to you young ones!"

"And what is that?" Marc was genuinely curious.

"You kidnap the brats. Ah yes, I am serious! you must kidnap your own children! Carry them off from their mothers, appropriate them! Be tactful—they may scratch, the mothers, they have a tigerish possessiveness for their cubs—but be resolute! Carry them off, habituate them to beards and tossings—and you will see, after her unexpected rest, how affectionate at eleven o'clock mama will be!"

"Aha!" said Marc, enlightened. "But—are *you* not too exhausted then?"

"Ah non! Only one hour you give them, and outside—or if they misbehave, off to bed, young, old, whatever! If they do not sleep, they must read, and reading is exercise for the mind. Besides, children are fascinating! Believe me, they have even been useful to me in my work!"

"Oh? And what work do you do?" Marc was feeling a strong affection for this expansive new acquaintance with the red hair and the snub nose; even François was beginning to think him worth cultivating.

"I am a policeman."

"You too?"

"And you!" It was established that Marc was of the Paris PJ, on holiday, and that Commissaire Jouvet was of the Sûreté Urbaine at Royan. As official bodies, the PJ and the Sûreté are not always on the best of footings, but this does not apply to holidays over a glass of white wine.

"Interesting, your job?"

"Ah yes, sufficiently. Nothing so exciting as you, of course, but"—he put a finger along his nose—"the tourists. Ah, you would not believe what they get up to, the tourists! The baggage lost, the wallet stolen, the wife in another's room, the holiday binge, the chauvinist brawl, the demolishing of landladies' rooms, the pissing upon public property! And it is I, Jouvet, who am the expert in tourists: I handle them all, soothe them, lecture them, and send them back to their homes in one piece if possible." By now they had moved, one beer and two sauternes replenished, to one of the wooden tables, and the scent of old wine rose from the floorboards at their feet. "Tourists on holiday *are* children . . . therefore, you see . . ."

"Ah," said Marc skeptically, "but will my children help me with my murderers? In my experience, it is I who turn murderer with them!"

"Then you do not go the right way about it. Parents, in my experience, are under the illusion—mistaken—that they must talk to their children. Fatal. To give lessons, impart moral tales, tell them how to behave—all fatal. One begins only with the smallest of questions. 'What did you do today?' 'How was school?' And then one listens. Uncritically. One must wait a long time, on occasions; but patience, answers will come. The child is like the criminal, he cannot abide silence. He begins to talk. And, as you say nothing, show no disapproval, he goes beyond talking, he gabbles, he ranges, he confides. Ah, then you learn! Human nature, the depths of its depravity! In the child's mind, it appears in its purest form —you learn who has stolen, who has looked under skirts, which of your children today hates which other enough to murder—after plumbing the soul of a child, to understand a thief, a rapist, a murderer is—child's play!" And he roared with laughter.

"And then what?" François was fascinated. "You tell him then, surely, where he has misbehaved—what his sins are?"

"No, not yet. After the sin comes the fear, and here you must listen most carefully. 'Papa, I did not mean to be tardy, but the dog on the corner snarls at me, so I go the long way round to avoid him.' 'Papa, I did not mean to hit Denise, but she is always picking on me, why doesn't she like me?' 'Papa, why are girls different?' 'Papa, is there really a God who will punish me if I stole even two francs from Jean's desk?' Then —then is your moment—that mind, that little touching spirit, lies open before you—and into it you let fall one drop, one drop only, of wisdom, of honor, which sinks deep as water into the thirsty soil. Of such moments, messieurs, is paternity made—but you must be oh so patient to capture them!"

So, when the women returned to the beach it was empty: at least of any of their appurtenances. "And he has even taken the blanket!" wailed Marie-Gisèle. "Well, I know just what I am going to do about it, I am going straight to shop for a beach towel. No, I ought not to be angry—here is my opportunity. I wanted to buy them before we left, but Marc said no, a blanket will do, and what's wrong with bath towels? Well, I ask you: from one end of the beach to the other, who is lying on an old flannel blanket that was on Pierre's bed until it got too tacky even for that? Men! And then we will go and have a cool cassis somewhere, that will show them!"

Laura was not unwilling: few things are more delightful than a shopping expedition on which you do not need anything and can therefore look at everything with a complaisant eye. The shops along the beach displayed everything from balloons guaranteed to pop as soon as a child looked at them to beach wraps and designer bikinis; what they did not have, it appeared, was towels, or only towels bearing such vulgar legends as SOUVENIR DE ROYAN, or JE CHAUFFE. Marie-Gisèle ended up paying more than she meant to, but "At least," she observed in the café, "Marc will not dare ask me, 'Why do you need it?' That is what irritates me more than anything else, when I say to Marc, 'I want to buy such-and-such,' and he never says 'Yes,' or 'We can't afford it this month,' but 'Why do you need it?' Tell me, how do you explain to a man why you MUST HAVE a coral lipstick?"

Laura laughed. It was not a problem she had had with her first husband, and François never thought about money. But with Paul, where both his generous funds and her own came under scrutiny, she had learned that having cash accountable to no one might literally mean life or death. "Yes, that is annoying . . . Is it more of a problem lately?"

Marie-Gisèle considered. "Well, it is more of a problem to *me*, because I feel that now Marc has advancement there are things we should be doing. Going out more, to meet people who can be of help to him—and I must have clothes, and the boys should have music lessons . . ."

"Do they want music lessons?"

"No, perhaps not . . . but it is important that they should have them."

"Why? Just to show off to the neighbors? Is this so important? If Marc is good at his job, it seems to me . . ."

"Oh no, my dear." Marie-Gisèle was rueful but decisive. "In America, perhaps, where a man is valued just for himself —but not in France. In France, I assure you, what the neighbors think is very important! And this is just what I cannot get him to see, that certain things we do not *need* are nevertheless critical—I have not even dared tell him I am looking for a better apartment!"

Laura considered; Marie-Gisèle was more likely to be right about this than she—and right or wrong, this frustration was making her unhappy. "But you begin at the wrong end," she said at last. "Don't ask, don't explain. Look, if Marc gave you a larger allowance, you could plan for yourself to afford these things, and it would cost no more in the long run, would it? *You* would do without this month, in order that next month . . . and I'm sure Marc doesn't enjoy being asked anymore than you enjoy asking! If you explained how much time it would save . . ."

"There! You *are* clever, Laura; I knew you would have a solution! I shall tell Marc I have done a time-cost study and this will be much more efficient—that this is how it is done in America!"

Laura laughed. "Don't you believe it! My mother complained of the very same thing, and it is her plan I have just given you!"

So it was in high good humor that wives and husbands reunited at the villa and decided to dine out this night; when one is on holiday, one wishes to sample all the local cuisine, and there was that little restaurant with the striped awning which specialized in seafood . . . When they came back, about nine, there was a small crowd by the steps—two reporters, a photographer—and Laura had opened her mouth to say, "No photographs, please," when she saw that their attention was focused—of course—on Jean Calvet. He stood at the top of the steps talking, it seemed, of the decline of the economy and the American recovery, and they were listening with attention. He was then perhaps a more important figure than she had thought—or perhaps August being a light month for news, the news gatherers had seen extra attractions in a trip to the seashore! His spectacular wife was not, however, in camera range; and after a moment Laura saw her off to the side in the garden, her eyes fixed on her husband in mingled anxiety and—what was it? fear? mourning? . . . Was he sometimes an unreliable speaker? He did not seem so. Or did there perhaps lie between them something deeper, more agonizing, than the common attraction of power and beauty? Such a man must be difficult to live with, used to his own way; possibly even pigheaded—and for the first time she felt for that self-assured goddess a kind of empathy.

They eased through the gathering, decided to take an after-dinner drink in the little salon across from the dining room. It was not quite uninhabited: the professor and his wife sat in one corner playing chess, and the journalist stood by the window. Laura asked him, with formal politeness, how his son was—had he gone to sleep normally? but he brushed her aside, almost like a sleepwalker; and she realized that his attention was, of course, on what Calvet was saying. Poor thing, would he take the fruits of his eavesdropping and make a story of his own of it? The villa was not exorbitant, but it was not cheap either, and the age of his suit did not mark him as prosperous.

The women knew all the staff now, having comforted Jacquot in the kitchen: the cook, the two waitresses cum chambermaids, and the man of all work who, neat in his white jacket, was now serving guests; and when he brought the cognac Laura asked, "Do you know the old woman who was in front this afternoon? Did she get home all right? She seemed rather . . ."

His gesture disposed of her, kindly. "Ah, our *Folle!* Yes, I saw her go, from the doorstep. She took a cab, though—*tiens,* that was unusual."

"A *Folle?*" inquired Marc, sipping, mildly and professionally interested. "Is she . . . ?"

"Oh, not at all dangerous, no, monsieur. It is her costume, mainly—she lives in the old days, and we are all used to her. She has a villa farther along and has lived there for years: there are many such here, living apart from life, you might say, and contemplating the sea which they will soon cross to the Isles of the Blessed."

"Figurez-vous! A poet!" and François raised his eyebrows.

"Oh, but that is an old belief, the Isles of the Blessed! Checkmate!" The professor picked up a bishop, glanced sideways to see whether the foursome was interested—and the men, lapped in postprandial indolence, were. "Celtic, you know—the dead went to the west, with the setting sun, and lived there in bliss on the Isles of the Blessed. Some think"— and, lifting his chair, he entered their circle—"that it means the Celts discovered America long before the Norsemen— Bran, a king of the Welsh or Irish, I forget which exactly, is said to have voyaged there. Myself, I doubt it; I think the concept is universal and as simple as the analogy with the setting sun."

"My husband," said his wife, joining them with a smile, "likes to talk."

"And is that your field, mythology?" François was curious.

"Ah no. I am a philologist—I search out the meaning of man in language. A chimerical quest, you may say, but in fact it is often most practical. It is language, for instance, which tells us what crops our ancestors grew and where—where smelting was first discovered—not so very long ago, either. We live as if our civilization was a taken-for-granted; but it is only ten thousand years old and we are still barbarians at heart, often."

Marc snorted agreement; and, "Is that why you came to Royan? to look at the sea?" Marie-Gisèle inquired, not entirely tactfully. He laughed. "No, we are not so old as that yet! We always holiday at the sea, there is a certain air of tranquility, of space; it is our first time here, however . . . But you must not say Royan, this is Pontaillac. Royan is that monstrosity down the road which the Germans wiped out for us and which has been rebuilt so as to prove we are now a race like them, enamored of technology and devoid of taste. Here, a more gracious age survives, villas and gardens are drenched in the air of a more eternal sea. And you? Is it your first visit?"

He was delighted to learn that it was, and deluged them with counsels of exploration. "La Rochelle, and Saintes—and you must go to the Ile, of course . . ." It was all very interesting, but Laura was tired and slipped away briefly to visit the ladies' room in the hall . . . it would be less crowded than in their common bathroom when they went up at last.

Someone else, invisible, was there when she entered the cubicle; and, in this strange room, in a strange town, in a strange way, she had a strange experience. The air grew cold, fatigue overwhelmed her; she thought of the Isles of the Blessed, of Paul, and it came to her how he had died, that François had killed him, and remembered for the first time in a long time that she slept every night with a murderer . . . A miasma of death, of despair, emanated from somewhere— perhaps even from someone . . . Powerfully she called upon her will to react, pushed open the door, forgetting her purse behind her. The door was just closing, and she breathed again. Even so, curious, she tugged on the heavy door to the hall . . . In the hall there was no one, but looking upward on the stairs she saw Madame Calvet ascending and, above her, the wife of the journalist.

CHAPTER 3

"A picnic on Oléron!" was the decision for the next day. Marie-Gisèle inquired if they should ask the kitchen for a lunch, but Laura said that with a sharp knife, salt, spoon, and a jar with a lid for butter you could eat anywhere—and fortunately she had brought these essentials. So, toward ten, they started out in François's car, which was the minimally larger of the two.

Marie-Gisèle had never heard of the island, and the men teased her, though Laura would have bet they could not have located it precisely until this spring either. They drove along the coast, past a series of curving graceful beaches framed by the elegant wistful arms of parasol pines; it would have been hot save for the sea breeze; and Marc exclaimed, "Who needs the Riviera? They have mimosa here too in the winter!" Laura sat forward—the women were in the backseat, of course—and cried, "Oh, I adore mimosa!" "So do I," said Marie-Gisèle practically, "but it makes me sneeze."

Drifting past marsh and field, they had no thought but for pleasure till Laura, seeing a farmer's back discreetly turned watering his furrow, was reminded of the curious sensations of last night's visit to the hall lavatory. "Those reporters last night—did they come all the way from Paris? Or does Calvet draw the local press because he lives near here?"

"No—near Poitiers somewhere but, *tu sais,* it's not so far off . . ." François, as might be expected, knew more of politics than the rest of them. "I don't know where the reporters came from, but the press likes him, he always gives them a quotable quote." Nothing there, it seemed, to cause his wife alarm—unless she was one of those women who did not like politics. "Have they children?"—a natural if not obvious train of thought. "No, they are too busy kissing them to have any." This was Marie-Gisèle. So . . . all the same she was convinced Mme. Calvet was not happy, and that, naturally, must be charged to her husband's account.

"How far is the Ile? Twenty miles? Less?" Marie-Gisèle did not like the unknown. "Is there a ferry? I hope I will not be seasick!" Marc laughed. "I promise you—on this ferry you will not be seasick!" And when they neared she saw why: a half-mile causeway linked the mainland to Oléron, its center span soaring to allow boat passage. "Why, we are nearly as high as the church steeple!" And indeed from the height of the bridge most of the island was visible, pale of sand and dark green of forest, the tall white steeple peaking in the distance as a landmark to ships at sea—and a strange network of man-made patterns on the east side. "First," said François, "we shall go to St.-Pierre and buy our picnic—then to the sights!"

They bought bread, butter, island-grown little tomatoes, Perrier and charcuterie; but, on their way back to the car, they were hailed by last night's guide, the professor. "So you came to Oléron as I suggested! Are you off to the oyster ponds? Let me guide you!"

Obediently they followed his car through the village to the dune highroad from whose modest slope an astonishing sight greeted them. As far as the eye could see, the marsh was caught into a raised patchwork counterpane of emerald fields hemmed by diamond streams and canals and dark velvet hedgerows, and sequined by tall-banked glistening oyster ponds. "But what do they *do?* How does one cultivate an oyster?" Marie-Gisèle wanted to know.

The professor was proudly proprietorial. "Ah, once they cultivated themselves—but mud, starfish, drills, and above all overdragging almost decimated them. It is a science now, and a tricky one. The seed is raised elsewhere—encouraged to fix itself on tiles or pickets laid out for the purpose—then, after a year, they are collected, all those tiny oysters, and brought here to these protected sea ponds to spend two years growing under the careful eye of the oystermen. You see their *cabanes* on each little property? Then they are harvested, thousands of tons of them, and slurp, down the gullets of Frenchmen!"

"So much—for so little!" Laura was not sure whether to mourn or admire.

"Yes, and much more than you see on this calm lovely day. The oysterman up to his knees in water at all seasons, the fluctuation of prices—and then a plague of starfish, an invasion of polluted water, and he is wiped out again."

"But it's not for so little!" Marc protested. "After all, an oyster! You must admit," he looked hungry, "there is something almost heavenly about an oyster."

"Well, we almost had none at all. When the Romans were here, the natural banks went all up the coast, you had only to take a basket . . . They enjoyed them as much as you, monsieur—grew them artificially in Lake Lucrinus in Italy, and it was so prosperous an affair Lucrinus took on the same meaning as—in your language, Madame Laura—filthy lucre!"

"Is that how you came to know so much about them? Lucre—Lucrinus?" He nodded, smiling. "I told you linguistics will take you to strange places." François regarded the gleaming ponds with sorrow. "I shall never," he said, "be able to eat an oyster again with quite the same nonchalance. An endangered species . . ."

"But if none of us ever ate any," observed Marie-Gisèle, practical as usual, "then no one would raise them, and they would certainly disappear."

"Ah yes, and the oyster, *mon vieux,* is an aphrodisiac! Think of that, and pay it the tribute of swallowing. And now I must leave you—I am off to the other side of the island to fish for those fish who have not yet been choked by the oil tankers."

They ate lunch a little way up the coast, in a forest of parasol pines whose cool *susurrements* calmed talk and left them enchanted and sleepy. Head back against a tree, François thought how rarely he and Laura had sat, two together, under the peace of solitary woods. Once, long ago, at Montargis when, on the banks of the canal, they had made love and parted, both too young to know what they were surrendering; once, three years since, when by a stream at Millau he had found her again. Well, she had not greatly changed since he first knew her, but she no longer plunged into passion or dislike; instead (the thought amused him) she sat slightly to one side and eyed reality, a cat wondering what to do with a cockroach.

And if, generous by nature, she had learned caution, no one could blame her; life had been liberal to her, but not kind. Curious: she was not in the least like Cécile, his first wife; that gentle nature had been manna to his spirit and he had drawn upon it ruthlessly. Laura was more intelligent than Cécile—highly intelligent and independent; yet in this marriage he felt himself the fountain of strength, that Laura had come home to him, trusting—when she at last made up her mind to do it—absolutely. It was a trust which mysteriously endowed him with the capacity to live up to it, and which he intended should be there for her to draw on forever; and, looking down at her head on his shoulder, he said gently, "Oh, *bonheur de ma vie,* however sleepy you may be, we came to Oléron to see lighthouses and beaches, not to drowse the afternoon away!"

And so they drove to the Pointe de Chassiron, with its black and white striped lighthouse and (after a breathless climb of more than two hundred steps) its magnificent view over the Ile de Ré, the Rock of Antioch, the Ile d'Aix; indeed over the whole coast from La Rochelle in the north, to Soulac and that long southern shore which led to Bordeaux, separated from them by the vast reach of the mouth of the Gironde. "Once," said François, sweeping an eloquent arm, "the sea covered all that we see, from the south of Brittany to the Massif Central and the Pyrénées, then the land rose; and every year we gain or lose a little more—a cliff crumbling there, a marsh filling here . . ." Marie-Gisèle shivered. "And Paris too? Was Paris beneath the sea?" He nodded. "It is, standing here," Laura marveled, "like riding the mast of a vast ship . . . I have never felt quite the same about the earth since they discovered it rides on plates above a molten mass; and every year the plates shift a little."

But the other side of the island cheered them: the immense beach on which Atlantic waves rolled tranquilly, and where from afar the professor and his boat were visible. He was not casting, however, but sitting chin on hand contemplating the sea. La Cotinière was a pretty port crammed with fishing sloops, sails flapping against the blue water and the fair sky: "Oh, I like this place," Marie-Gisèle exclaimed. "It has everything an island should have: charming houses, waves, beach, forest, vegetables, and oysters! I could stay here forever! And you, Laura?" Laura shook her head, smiling. "You see—Franchot is on the other side of that bridge, and if it crumbled . . ." "Ah." "And speaking of oysters," remarked Marc, "shall we?" Gladly, they took seats in a port-side bistro and ordered a dozen each; nor did François hesitate to swallow them.

"Tiens—we are not the only visitors from the villa," and Marie-Gisèle pointed to where, along the quay, the journalist walked, his wife ahead and Jacquot well ahead of her—running and, as Marie-Gisèle observed, nearly tumbling into the water. "That boy," observed François, "is not long for this world," and—it was not his son!—returned his attention to his oysters. But Laura continued to watch as mother caught boy, and father caught mother by the arm, angrily, saying something no doubt about keeping a closer eye on him. But she rounded on him as angrily, and her voice rose. *"Et si je suis folle . . ."* something unheard *"tu l'es autant de la craindre!"* A curious phrase: to fear whom, or what? the feminine pronoun in French is subject to so many interpretations. Fear Jacquot's death by drowning? her own imprudence? the landlady's bill?—At any rate, there seemed to be more than one uneasy couple at the villa!

They drove home in the transparent stillness of evening, blissful and pleasantly weary; but as they entered the hall with its black and white floor tiles a large man, red and untidy against so much elegance, rose to meet them. *"Tiens!"* said Marc. "It is our friend, François, Commissaire Jouvet of Royan. Well, *mon ami*, is this a social visit, or are your intentions purely criminal?"

Jouvet looked at once friendly and grave. "The latter, alas." He drew them gently just inside the empty dining room. "I regret to say that we have had a murder in Royan—the murder of an old lady—they call her the Folle de Pontaillac." Laura exclaimed and he looked at her curiously.

"And you are"—Marc was puzzled—"looking for me?"

"No, not yet. At the moment"—and he turned to François in apology—"I am seeking your friend, l'avocat de Paris!"

CHAPTER 4

"Her lawyer!" said François unbelieving, regarding the packet tied with blue ribbon on which, above the printed "Will," spidery lines in green ink traced the legend, "Pour François LeBreton de Paris, mon avocat."

They were standing, Marc, he and Jouvet, by the charming little escritoire in the salon of the Madwoman's villa, furnished in that Louis XV style which had once been mandatory for those aspiring to elegance. His utter disbelief might have surprised one who did not know that in France it is a notary who deals with wills, while a lawyer proper handles only cases which come to court. Marc and Jouvet, however, understood him; and "You have been busy here," observed Marc, noting that the bills, letters, string, stamps, and elastic bands which had been the escritoire's contents lay scattered upon its leaf.

"It is as we found it. No, do not touch; it will be dusted for prints when that idiot Sarrazin gets himself out of bed. It is inconvenient, sometimes, to have only a small staff, and he is the only one whose fingers are not all thumbs, or covered with jam—The point is, what can you tell me about this lady?"

"I have never heard of her before in my life that I know," said François forcibly. "What was her real name, then?"

"According to her postman, Edith Lemay—but her passport, which is also in this heap somewhere, says Annette Frejon."

"Neither—neither one nor the other has ever been a client or known to me in any other way." He shook his head. "No, you may doubt, but I have a good memory."

Jouvet gave him a glance, ironic but not unfriendly. *"Vrai?"* Marc interposed. "Take it as true for the moment—he will, of course, check later, and what reason she had for consigning her will to him will no doubt become clear. You have noticed, however, that the ink on that note is recent and of a different color to that on the will itself?"

Jouvet nodded approvingly. "How fresh, we cannot tell—I have not studied the will yet, being more occupied with its position and the fact that it has apparently been untied recently. Now we replace it exactly as it was"—his fingers, wrapped in a clean handkerchief, were delicate—"and await Sarrazin and the photographer, who is now developing the photos of the corpse as we found it. Here," and he led the way to the hall, "is where it lay when the mailman saw it through the door pane on his afternoon rounds. I need not tell you to keep your fingers to yourself."

Marc looked at the hall with interest: it was narrow and considerably dingier than the salon, an umbrella stand with an old raincoat hanging on a rack above its only furnishings. A small dark stain was barely visible against the aged patina of the floorboards: "Bullet? Knife? Blunt instrument?" he inquired.

"The latter—blows to the head, perhaps a dozen, but we have not found the weapon; it appears to have been slightly curved." He took a half step forward from the doorway, gesturing. "She lay *so*, head facing the salon, feet pulled up under her dress hem; her face was unrecognizable, but the rest . . . If it were not for the search, I would have no hope of fingerprints; it looks as if she answered the door and was struck down instantly. No doubt it was after dark last night, but the pathologist will tell us."

"And then whoever it was searched the house. The salon, at least. That tells us something."

"Oh yes." Jouvet was ironic. "Violence and burglary."

"A little more than that. Your ordinary burglar, I imagine, would have made entry at the back or through the cellar; she would have surprised him somewhere else than here. This one was bold."

"The hedge in front is thick, from the street no one could see him."

"Nevertheless *I* would have begun at the back. And he came ready for violence—there is nothing he could snatch up here, unless . . ." he craned forward. "Well, I suppose there might have been an umbrella or a cane in the umbrella rack. Even so—she opened the door to him, and there was no initial struggle; any fight, and I am sure that coat would have fallen, the rack is not very stable. What is missing?"

Jouvet shrugged. "How can we know till we know what was once here? It was always a magpie's nest, this house, the neighbors tell me—china figures, photos in silver frames, paintings—all that we know for sure is that the trinket cabinet in the dining room is half-empty, and a pin which she always wore at the neck of her dress was torn off—the rent was visible. A ring, perhaps, too—it looks as if she wore one. Ah, that will be a fine inventory, searching the house—you should see her bedroom! and the kitchen! she may have eaten occasionally—there is only an old cheese in the larder—but she washed dishes once a month if ever!"

"Still, it tells you what to look for—a thief who habitually uses violence—and who has probably been around for a few days. He must, it seems to me, have known her by sight, seen her jewelry, knew that she lived alone—he may even have followed her home. Are you planning to call in the PJ?"

Jouvet's grin was wicked. "What, with you around?" But, seeing Marc's look of anguish, "No, no, don't upset yourself. A robbery with violence is certainly, I think, within the capacity of the Sûreté Urbaine—but when I report to divison I hope I have your permission to say—humm?"

Marc hesitated; he knew exactly what Jouvet meant. He was confident of a quick solution which would be a feather in his cap, and having Marc on tap was an excellent defense against having the case taken away from him. "Well," he agreed reluctantly, "yes—but remember, both M. LeBreton and I will be very unhappy if anything is to interfere with our lying quietly in the sun."

"I promise to remember—though M. LeBreton has already in some sense the obligation to assist us. And I hope he will be able to do so more than he already has! But here is Sarrazin." And, gesturing through the window, he went to the back door to admit the fingerprint man, followed by a neat and gloomy, suited figure laden with camera and flash. "Well, my friend," he touched Sarrazin upon the shoulder, "I hope your little girl is still doing well?" "Yes, thank you, chief; the fever broke early this morning and we felt we could sleep finally about ten." Jouvet's strictures on sleepy crews and jammy fingers were, evidently, a sort of reverse pride for outside consumption only, for he regarded the tousled young man with affection and shoved him into the salon.

"Dust the bureau, the door to the hall, the outside door, the hall itself—and then anywhere a searcher may have touched. Ah yes, and don't forget the banister leading upstairs! As for you, Maréchal, we want photographs of the desk and of all the rooms—it will take some study to decide what is the usual disorder and what if anything is not! And follow Sarrazin, cretin, don't go ahead, so we can be sure you have not touched anything!"

The photographer, apparently quite used to this form of address, grinned sourly and sketched a salute; Jouvet escorted his two guests out by the back door by which they had come. "As for you, lawyer, I will send you the will as soon as we finish with it—next-of-kin has not been notified yet, and you may be of some use with that—or other things, once you have reflected a bit!" And his grin was that of a bulldog who sees, from the corner of his eye, the postman's pants flapping up the walk.

Laura, watching François go, was obscurely uneasy, as if he walked into danger; which was odd, for not so long ago it had been she who walked in danger, not he. Yet the uneasiness was there—because, probably, their holiday had been interrupted by a sudden and violent event; it was a time when one's instinct was to huddle inward, to keep together. She took Marie-Gisèle's arm, tucked it under her own. They had had sandwiches after the oysters, and the diners were just finishing at the villa, but she was suddenly hungry. "If we went into the salon—had coffee and some rich desserts?" "Oh yes! a splendid idea! Since Marc has abandoned me, I might as well get fat!"

The journalist and his wife were already there when they entered, arguing fiercely. "I tell you, there is absolutely no reason to . . ." but she, the wife, fell silent as they came in. Jean the jack-of-all-trades pushed open the swinging door at the rear that led to the kitchen premises. "Mesdames?" "Can we have coffee, and if you have any, *pâtisserie*?" "*Sur l'instant.*"

The journalist looked at them uneasily. "You have had a good day?" "Oh yes, until now—and you? We saw you on Oléron." This seemed to disconcert him extremely, and his wife leaped into the breach. "A charming place, is it not?" "Very charming, and Jacquot? He has recovered?" She accepted this topic of conversation with enthusiasm. "Oh yes, he enjoyed the beach; the doctor, as you saw, thought a butterfly bandage would do and there will be no scar, he says." She was one of those dark women who cannot be still, and her dress, low in the bosom, splashed flowers rather brighter than Laura would have worn. Polyester, too, which did not hang well in warm weather—not a prosperous pair. Her husband essayed a false and bonhomous smile. "Luckily for him, and more than he deserves—but he is a boy, of course, and boys are always getting into trouble, aren't they?"

Laura opened her mouth to say that, having one of her own, she hoped not; but Jean returned, setting down coffee cups with a flourish and tarts entirely filled with walnut cream. "Ah! Comfort, Marie-Gisèle—they say sugar is good for shock, don't they?" Jean, hovering napkin on arm, watched her eat with satisfaction. "Ah, you mean the old lady! I saw the policeman when he asked for you. A terrible thing, one is not even safe in one's old age these days, it appears! And to think that just yesterday we spoke of her nearing the Blessed Isles . . ." he looked sad.

"Did you know her, Jean? Was she a nice old lady?" Laura wanted to know.

"Ah. We all knew her, of course, to see, at any rate! One could not miss her. As for nice, I would say so—always polite, and there was no harm in her, you understand." Laura understood; in a world where one was constantly assailed by the egos of others, someone who had no harm in her was pleasant to know. "She was, of course, excitable about some things. When there were films or performances she did not approve, she would write to the newspaper. One day, I remember, a woman on the beach was tanning and had taken off her bikini top. She expressed herself to me—I was on the steps—very strongly. People thought nothing of this sort of thing, she said, but it was truly most serious: 'In our youth we are careless, but in our maturity we pay the penalty.' It was quite impressive. She also felt strongly about the manners of children: when they made fun of her, she threatened them with her umbrella. Nor did she like dogs much. But for the most part, just a harmless old lady."

"Nice, apart from not liking children and dogs," said Marie-Gisèle, with a dimple of irony. "Well, we can hardly expect the insane to be nicer than the rest of us, can we?"

The professor, who had just entered with his wife and was heading for the chess table, looked round. "What is this? Who is insane? Not myself, I hope!"

"No, no, it is an old woman," said the journalist's wife eagerly, "who was murdered last night."

"Murdered! Good God. My dear," turning to his wife, "we must be careful. If they are victimizing the old, even here in Royan, we may be next!"

She had paled, but she smiled even so. "No—I am sure this is a peaceful place for the most part—is it not so, Jean?"

"Oh, assuredly, madame. And a murder—except for the

wife of the butcher, who assailed him with one of his cleavers and then went off with the meat inspector—we have not had a murder in twenty years."

"And did the inspector inspect the cadaver before they departed?" "No, madame, he was buying the train tickets." "Well there, you see? I am sure the circumstances in this case also were unusual: the lady was not, after all, your ordinary seaside visitor." Laura's tone was consoling. "What kind of life had she led, Jean? I don't even know her name."

"Oh, for her life, madame, she came here perhaps twenty years ago, and of what went before I cannot inform you at all. But her name—yes, I believe her name was Edith Lemay."

The professor's hand flew up and the chessboard toppled. "Sorry, my dear—clumsy of me." He bent to pick up the pieces and raised a flushed face to the onlookers. "No, just for a moment I thought . . . it sounded familiar, but then, it is a rather theatrical name, isn't it? Meg Villars, Jane Marnac, Willy . . ."

"You are babbling, my dear," said his wife, warning. "But *tiens!* it is sad. Have the police any idea who did it?" The Calvets, at the door to the salon, finding all the seats occupied, paused before turning away, shoulder to shoulder as usual, a closed corporation. "Ask the ladies," said the journalist's wife in sudden malice: "the commissaire was here and went off with both their husbands." Laura met the sudden attack with dignity. "I do not know why the commissaire wanted my husband, but he is a lawyer, so . . ."

"And mine"—Marie-Gisèle had not intended to make this public, but instinct sent her to Laura's defense—"is an inspector of the Police Judiciaire."

It was, for a second, the two of them back to back against the rest; but from which point of the compass came the sudden intensity, the sharpening of hostile interest, Laura could not tell.

CHAPTER 5

At the Villa Brise de Mer, they did not serve breakfast trays: the dining room was much more convenient than running up and downstairs. It was at breakfast next morning, therefore, that François expatiated at length to his friends on his injuries. He was not easy to irritate, Laura thought, watching him; but it was in his nature to be irritable. Now Paul, her last husband, had not been irritable—but then, she recalled with surprise, when *Paul* was irritated he might kill you! Some spring snapped open within her, and she laughed: a sound so delightful that François paused in midcourse and resumed more reasonably, *"Mais voyons!* it is not really amusing to have a stupid old woman mistake a lawyer for a notary and leave one open to suspicion in a murder case! Next time I go on holiday, I shall take a false name—François Villon, that will show them!"

Marc shook his head and took a bite from his croissant. "He does not really suspect you," he said tolerantly. "It is just that —he is not certain yet it was a simple robbery. Oh yes! I watched him yesterday when I was pointing out what might not fit, and he had thought of all those things already. He wants it to be simple, you see, because then he can solve it simply; but in case it is not, he keeps me on the string and you too, feeling you may have useful things to tell him. And I am not sure he is wrong."

François was affronted. "I would lie in a case of this gravity?"

"No; but it is still possible that you knew her, that you will still remember . . . A person with two names, that suggests that somehow, somewhere, she may have had something to do with the law."

Laura and Marie-Gisèle looked at one another and laughed. "Well?—You don't think so." Marie-Gisèle glanced at Laura. "The theater, we think—don't we, Laura? just as the professor said."

"It does seem likelier. The costume . . ."

"Ah." Marc digested this. "Quite possibly. People in the limelight are apt to think that of course one has heard of them—and, likewise, to take a special interest in others' notoriety. It would not be a simple mistake, then, that . . ."

"No one mistakes an *avocat* for a *notaire,*" Marie-Gisèle was firm, "not even a peasant. And she could write! Her will . . ."

"It may be then, you think, that she remembered François' name from the newspapers? Wanted a famous man—a kind of vanity?"

"It was a message." Laura was certain. "It is too early to tell yet what it means exactly; but it was a message."

As required, Jouvet reported the death of Edith Lemay to the regional PJ, but when it came up at morning conference it received scant heed. Bombs in Paris—the Israeli-PLO war carried to the banks of the Seine! Were there terrorists too in Nantes and La Rochelle? What did the SDECE say? Precautions to be taken occupied most of their time. "For information only—Jouvet is asking for comparable MOs, men with a record of robbery with violence. And if it turns out to be more than that, he says he has a PJ man from Paris there on holiday, homicide squad!"

One of the inspectors laughed. "A policeman's holiday . . ."

"Now, here is something we must send out a flier about. We have had reports from other districts this summer, and here is a new one from Dinan, of a young man preying on older women. Seducing them, I suppose, though it's not that explicit; and then he goes off with their jewelry, whatever is lying handy, and when they object threatens to tell their husbands. You know as well as I do, if we have"—the commissioner shuffled his papers—"seven cases reported, there must have been a dozen that were not. He seems to specialize in older women on their own, and . . ."

"What? two dozen in one summer? *Mon Dieu,* what a capacity!"

The Commissioner replied with a wintry grin. "Well, perhaps he works them in tandem! At any rate we must catch him. Circulate a description—dark hair and dark eyes, thirtyish, handsome—with particular attention to resort areas, he seems to prefer them." And that for the moment was all that was said about Edith Lemay.

For the first time in their stay, the weather was less than ideal for a holiday: it was not raining, but dampness threatened, and serried dark clouds rolled in from the Atlantic: "A city day!" said François "If we went to explore La Rochelle?" Your Parisian is an eclectic creature; just as the New Yorker will fly to Acapulco before he has visited Chicago, the inhabitant of Paris will have toured Italy, London, Amsterdam, even—God forbid!—Brussels before he makes the acquaintance of Rouen or Poitiers: none of them had ever seen La Rochelle. *"Tiens, une bonne idée,"* said Marie-Gisèle, "The siege of La Rochelle—I remember that from the history books!"

"Yes—but these days I expect it will be full of the professor's oil tankers," Marc warned gloomily.

There were tankers, but there was also romance. As they looked out over the immense harbor complex, with its basins for commerce, fishing and pleasure boating, its tangle of masts, funnels, sails, none but was impressed by the sense of the majesty of trade, of how tangled and tantalizing were the highroads of the sea. And the past lingered, brooding: the Tour de la Lanterne and the medieval *donjons* flanking the port, challenged the gray clouds with their pinnacles and crenellations, evoking still the days when La Rochelle was the stronghold of French Protestantism, unassailable until Richelieu blockaded the harbor and starved the proud city into submission. Back from the quays, in narrow alleys, wooden houses with outthrust beams and carved bay panels stubbornly resisted four hundred years of storm and weathering; overhanging balconies, arcaded porches where the walker could skulk from the elements, breathed still an ancient air of refuge. *Mais c'est tout à fait romanesque!"* exclaimed Marie-Gisèle. "Never have I seen a place so old."

"Not in Paris? not down by the Seine—the rue St.-André-des-Arts or the Chat-qui-Pêche?" But she had not; her daily shopping rounds had simply never taken her there. They walked and wondered, a medieval seaport coming alive for them . . . "But I smell," said Laura suddenly, "something exotic. Molasses? Vanilla? Spice? They call it the Geneva of the north—then why am I suddenly thinking of Amsterdam?"

"A profound and historic sense of smell." François was amused. "Oh yes—if Amsterdam brought the East Indies to Europe, La Rochelle brought the West—they had vast plantations once in the Caribbean."

"Ah! This is more like Geneva!" They had emerged from the old city into the eighteenth century, streets a little wider, classic stone mansions behind gardens and gates and balustraded walls where, here and there, jutted an urn, a lion's head, a Corinthian capital. Marie-Gisèle's nose sniffed. "I smell—the haute bourgeoisie, wax and parquet floors . . ."

"Brocaded furniture and velvet drapes . . ." suggested Laura.

"Six-course meals—paneled dining rooms . . ."

"Testered beds—and even now maids to make them."

"Arranged marriages, weddings of property, and"—she sneezed violently—"dust!"

"Astonishing, what a woman can smell!" The men jeered, but they were inpressed, all the same. A guidebook was purchased at an ancient librairie, sandwiches were purchased at a bistro and (the sun was now very nearly visible) they absorbed physical and mental nourishment in that vast park where once the city's defensive walls stood . . . It was a short break in the weather, however, and three o'clock found them racing for shelter in a warm and uncrowded café of the last century, all mahogany and gilt-bordered mirrors. "Well now—these Protestants—" Marie-Gisèle slipped the rain hood from her dark head—"what were they protesting? Remind me."

It was a large question, but François was only momentarily taken aback. "Well—in the beginning, of course, church abuses: the buying of bishoprics, nepotism, illiterate curés, church wealth, while the peasants were starving—and good Catholics protested too, so that the church itself underwent reformation. Those who were not convinced of its sincerity, however, broke away, and in France fought for religious freedom under Henry of Navarre among others—you remember 'Paris is worth a mass?' "

Marie-Gisèle nodded promptly. "He converted, and we got Henry IV and religious tolerance. What then?"

"Then, sometime later, came Richelieu, who thought France would be neater to govern if we had the same faith as well as the same king. This time, no Henry IV, the war was lost, and thousands of skilled Protestant workers fled to England, Holland, Switzerland—all very wasteful to us and profitable to them!"

Marie-Gisèle nodded vigorously. "Yes, especially as I suppose what came of it in the end was the Revolution and state atheism! One would have thought"—Marie-Gisèle was the kind of Catholic who goes faithfully to mass as long as her children are impressionable, then gives it up in favor of sleeping in of Sundays—"the first thing their religion would have taught both sides was not to kill people!"

Marc laughed, a little bitterly. "How about the Arabs and the Israelis? The Sunnis and the Shiites?—Three centuries ago twenty-three thousand people starved here—men, women, and children—during Richelieu's siege. As someone once said, 'The first thing a powerful idea does is to kill someone.' "

She made a moue, disapproving. "Well at least we know better than that nowadays. In France at any rate no one cares anymore what is your religion. Or even if you have one!"

"Yes, but I'm not so sure that . . ." François frowned. "We're tolerant, certainly, but perhaps that's just because we don't care very much for anything. Let people do their own thing, we say, and pride ourselves on our tolerance; does it matter as long as others stay out of our way? *Fais ce que voudras*, in Rabelais' phrase, freedom is all . . . and yet I wonder. Is anything ever so simple? whatever we think, everything is *not* possible."

Laura, chin on hands, watched her husband with interest. It was as if they were students again, young and intent upon the Idea, which alone had any reality, and she blessed the unfamiliar ambience, the cozy fug, the relaxed intimacy which had lured him to talk of things he would normally never put into words.

"And what does that mean?" asked Marie-Gisèle.

"It means that if we have laissez-faire parents we have children with no self-discipline; and if we throw away sexual inhibitions we get herpes II. The wages of sin is death, the sins of the fathers will be visited upon the children even to the fourth generation—the old Protestants really believed all that, you know! We—I at least—revolted: if God is like that, an old man with a whip for me if I am so careless as to say *merde*, I can't believe in him."

"And now? You do believe?" Marie-Gisèle was curious, not quite incredulous.

"Now, I am older, and I observe that these sayings are often quite true. There is a law, very remotely related to the law I serve, but a law all the same, that makes them true, ineluctable. The sins of the fathers *are* visited upon the children, however innocent they may be—ask any doctor, any psychologist, any notary! As for the wages of sin—look at the whore with syphilis, the drunkard and his liver! But there are subtler effects still—when we live as we please, self-indulgent, our own pleasures become our obsessions, our torments —some inner crumbling . . . I cannot describe what I mean, but I see it every day: the man who is shrunken in, incapable of joy, eaten up by his mistresses, his horse races, his business . . . The wages of sin *is* death, and perhaps after all it is better to kill and be killed for something more important, something worth believing in. But now," he looked at his watch, "the rain is not letting up, and perhaps it is time to go back."

"Yes," agreed Marie-Gisèle. "I did want to see the Aquarium, but this is a bit too much like being in one!"

Madame the landlady, on the watch and coiffure at the majestic ready, waited for them in the front hall of the Villa Brise de Mer. "Here," and she put it into François's hands, "is a packet for you from the police, they brought it an hour ago and told me to give it only into your hands and so I have given it!" She dusted her own, metaphorically shaking police soil from their long-nailed elegance. "I feel," said Marc as they went up the stairs, "that friends of the police are perhaps non grata in this establishment. They are honest people, though—like Marie, I can smell it in the furniture polish!"

But François was too busy breaking the seal on the envelope to answer, and as they crowded into the bedroom, he detached a note in Jouvet's ham-handed fist. "We have taken all needed prints (and, as you might expect, found nothing) so the will is now the executor's to execute. No address for the heir anywhere in the will or the house and of course I as well as you would very much like to know where he is. And was? And I think you will have something to tell me when you have read the codicil. Yours in haste, Jouvet."

Anxious, they watched as François unfolded the paper, its stiff creases attesting its age. "I, Annette Frejon, *dite* Edith Lemay . . . Well, at least she uses both names, so it may just be valid . . ,"

"It also suggests she had nothing sinister to conceal," said Marc.

"Just so." He glanced down it. "All that she owns to her 'nephew Jacques,' no last name, may the devil fly off with her! Except for two other bequests, something to a home for retired actors, and a gift to a convent school in Marseille with which to buy books on acting and great actresses! Now what is that, gratitude or . . . mischief?"

"Mischief," said Marie-Gisèle, standing on tiptoe to read it herself. "We said theater, didn't we say that, Laura, this morning!"

"You did—And that's all, signed and dated eight years ago, witnessed by the postman, who has included his profession; and, I suppose, a neighbor. Imprecise, handwritten, exasperating, but as far as I can see, perfectly legal. But where is this codicil?"

"There." Laura pointed.

He turned the sheet over; improbably, a bit of yellow foolscap, also handwritten, was stapled to the back. He read aloud the fresh green-inked handwriting, unwitnessed, certainly invalid: "And to the *wife* of my lawyer, Laure LeBreton, my emerald pendant."

CHAPTER 6

"Absolument impossible!" Laura said it firmly, and then tried it over in English. "Ab-so-lute-ly impossible!" She might as well say it: everyone else had. *"Absolument impossible"*—François to Jouvet at his postbreakfast arrival for a conference in the villa salon—"impossible that I should have had anything to do with her and forgotten it." *"Absolument impossible"*—Jouvet to François—"that she should have left her will to your care—and to your wife an emerald pendant! unless there is some connection." "I assure you, Commissioner, I did not know her from Adam." "Or Eve—" Marie-Gisèle's not very helpful contribution.

Only Marc had not said it; fixing Jouvet with a steady and not unfriendly warning glance, he observed, "M. LeBreton, you know, is an extremely well-known lawyer—and both he and his wife were much in the news at the time of the Monnet affair. So, faced with so many impossibilities, should we not concentrate instead upon the possible? The circumstances of her death? . . . After all, we four all have alibis, even though only our spouses can vouch for us."

There was a silence in the little salon, abandoned by the other residents of the Brise de Mer, who no doubt felt like madame that the police were not desirable acquaintances. Laura looked out, past the dim portieres, to where brilliant asters and dahlias sparkled against the sharp green of privet and, beyond it, the calm gravity of the sea: like a soul's progress from the Folies-Bergère to heaven . . . Jouvet mastered his temper. "Very well. But I would still like to know why her mind fixed on you—and your wife on top of that—

especially as we have not found any pendant, emerald or otherwise!" And the door did not quite slam behind him.

Troubled, they mounted the stairs to the Taverniers' room, which having a view over the beach lent to a perspective. Laura and Marie-Gisèle took the chairs, Marc lay on the bed, frowning, and François, forehead to pane, said wearily, "I cannot tell you how disconcerting, and how tedious, I find all this! Marc, you do not really believe I am concealing some knowledge of this woman, do you?"

Marc hesitated, searching his own mind straightforwardly. "No. I think that when we learn the whole, the explanation will be perfectly simple, but it is not the kind of explanation one gets directly. So there is no point in getting obsessed with our little mystery; but it would be foolish to ignore it either. Jouvet does not really suspect you, but there are too many curious things here for him not to question . . . and my connection with the PJ does not help. On the one hand, he is determined to show me he can do his job as well as I could; on the other, he knows just how easily I could pull the wool over his eyes if I chose! I sympathize with him, and I think it would help if we came up with *some* answers . . . We do not know why she made you her executor or left Laura this necklace which may or may not exist; but we do know when—very recently. What have you or Laura done lately that might catch her attention?"

Laura exclaimed. "She saw us!—Well, she saw me, you were still on the beach, I think, François. Perhaps, after all, it was the sight of me that startled her!"

The men had not yet heard of this incident; now Laura and Marie-Gisèle described it, the pause in front of the villa, the old woman's shock, her hand to her heart, the flower seller's anxiety . . . "Good—just what we need to know. She saw you, she recognized you from your photographs in the paper, she remembered possibly also that your husband was a lawyer. What it does not explain is why at that moment this was important to her. After all, one does not just see a lawyer's wife on the street and remember one's will needs an executor—and not a notary, mind you, but a lawyer!"

"There was something else," Marie-Gisèle said suddenly. "She was already worried, and . . . Laura, or François, meant something in that context. A spy? She had discovered a spy in Pontaillac?"

"A spy? In Pontaillac? Spying on what?" Marc's laugh dismissed it.

"It need not have been a spy." Laura defended her fellow female. "It could have been anything. She had been followed on the street, perhaps, or thought she was; after all she was old and I suppose not quite sensible. She was afraid, and seeing us—it was a kind of protection, to call our attention to her."

Marc examined this and was not dissatisfied. "Yes, it might have been. Two points, though. Jouvet says she probably opened the door to her murderer—the neighbors say normally it was locked day and night. If she was frightened, why did she? The other point is even stickier—if she was really worried about something, why did she not simply call the police, or write it down for us—why play games with wills and mythical emerald necklaces?"

"She didn't want to appear a fool." Marie-Gisèle spoke decisively. "You know, Marc, connections sometimes only make sense indirectly. Do you remember the day your mother arrived unexpectedly, and I walked in carrying her favorite madeleines in my bag? 'You're psychic,' she said— she was really impressed by that. But it was only that I saw some geraniums almost as splendid as hers in a window box, and I was on my way to the *pâtisserie* anyway, so when I walked in subconsciously I just chose them . . . The same thing here, in all probability. Something caused her unease, but she could not define it. Seeing Laura, François, gave her comfort, but she could not define that. Fear made her think of death, death of wills, she made a gesture—the LeBretons on my will will protect me."

It made a kind of sense, psychologically; Marc nodded.

"But can we then not find out what upset her?" François was curious.

Marc shook his head. "That is Jouvet's job—and I'm sure he is doing it. All the same, François, there is another direction in which you might be helpful—one I expect he has not yet thought of."

"What?"

"The heir, that nephew who is one of the countless Jacques's in France and the territories! If his name is Frejon, Jouvet will find him—but suppose he's a sister's son? It may take forever to locate him, especially since we do not yet have, like the Americans and the Germans, computers to tell us everything. But the will itself gives you a pointer to your legatee."

"How?"

"The nuns' school in Marseille. She attended it, almost certainly. It was a long time ago—but nuns have long memories, and good ones. Supposing you drop them a line—see if someone remembers her, her brothers and sisters?"

Jouvet, back at the office, simmered. On the one hand, simple robbery with violence; on the other, a Guignol tangle of Paris lawyers, missing heirs, and emerald necklaces. And a PJ man too! A nice fellow, now if he belonged to the Sûreté one might quite like him! But at the moment, it was the last thing he needed. Well, he knew which he preferred it to be, and with luck he could prove it. In his ten years in Royan he could remember only five murders; all but one he had solved successfully—and that one the PJ had made a *merde* of. It was not their fault, exactly; they had not known enough about your stubborn Poitou peasant to arrest Marcel Blanc for shooting his brother before he had shot, also, his wife, two children, and himself; but it still rankled a little. This one would be, if he had his way, solved by him too, and solved simply: "Sarrazin!" He went to the door. "Do you know yet what our local bouquet of cow thistles have been up to?"

Sarrazin rose and trotted into the office. "Almost, chief."

He consulted one of the papers he carried. "Alain and Geoffroy have good alibis—well, Alain's is only his wife but she's a good girl and she wouldn't lie about it. Michelet is in Saintes, visiting his sister, and has been for a week—but it's tricky to pin down his movements on the night in question. Sonzac is on holiday in Bordeaux, and I've asked Bordeaux to give him the once-over."

Jouvet grunted. "Policemen work, and thieves take a holiday—that's how it is nowadays. What about Albert, then? I like him, he's just stupid enough to walk up to an old lady's front door, say 'Give me your jewels,' and panic when she opened her mouth to yell."

"Albert's in jail in La Rochelle, chief, since Saturday."

"Really? What a pity. Or, rather, splendid! What's he been up to?"

"Breaking and entering, and maybe a few other charges . . . Seems a jeweler died last week, and a friend of his in the district said, 'Come up and break a safe with me.' They picked the night of the funeral, of course, knowing nobody would be near the shop—but as it happened, there was a retirement party at the *pâtisserie* next door, people eating brioches and drinking champagne, so they didn't dare blow the safe on the premises. 'Well, let's haul it away,' says the friend. His brother has a garage just a couple of blocks from there. So they manhandle it to the door, and heave it down the steps, and pant and push it along the sidewalk."

"Ha!" A faint rumble of anticipation encouraged Sarrazin to continue. "I can just see Albert, lazy slob, I hope he strained every muscle . . . So then?"

"Well, while they're doing it, along comes a *flic*—a young one, not up to the mark yet, and says, 'Can I help you?' " A snort. "Oh yes, red faces! but I ask you, chief, who would expect two safebreakers to trundle their loot openly in the street? . . . So what could they say but yes, and . . ."

Two snorts and a gurgle. "The three of them? Heaving it down the road? *Vrai?*"

Sarrazin nodded, conspiratorial. "All three . . . And it

went fine till the last half-block . . . that was on a slope, you see, and the safe had wheels, and . . . Well, Albert was fool enough to run around in front, try to stop it . . . It pinned him to the wall, of course; his friend panics and starts to run and the cop, finally, begins to think there's something peculiar . . ." But Jouvet was laughing too hard to hear him. "And then? And after?"

"They rescued Albert and put him in jail. But they're not sure yet they can charge him with robbery, because when they opened the safe—they had a terrible time getting it up the steps to the station, they told me—it was empty except for a dead cat . . . All the stock had gone to the bank already, but the family pet had died, and they were keeping it there—no air, you see—till they could get to the taxidermist . . ."

Jouvet, chest heaving, bent over the desk, waved a feeble hand for him to be silent. "No more—ah—and all for nothing —a dead cat—if I could only have been there to see Albert's face when they opened it!" He pulled out a handkerchief, wiped his eyes, blew his nose, and returned to business. "So— you'll keep on at Sonzac? Michelet?—Ah, but Sarrazin—a good laugh is worth getting up for in this business!—Do we know anything yet about the weapon?"

"Not much. The doctor says narrow, with a slight curve to it, and we haven't found anything . . . But he puts the time of death between nine-thirty and twelve, with a preference for the earlier side . . ."

Jouvet's brows went up. "That early! Why, it would scarcely have been dark yet!"

"I know, but that's what he says. He also says he found bits of something in the wound, they've gone to the lab to be analyzed . . . You saw the lawyer this morning, chief; did you get anything?"

Jouvet's features collapsed into a dense frown. "Nothing— never saw her, never heard of her. And what is worse, *ami*, it seems this lawyer fellow is pretty well known, he and his wife were prominent in the Monnet affair—I knew that name meant something! So our madwoman may well just have read his name in the papers . . . Which does not prevent it from being suggestive, all the same, especially—what are we doing about the old bat's emerald necklace, if she had one?"

"Well, we know it's not in the house—but then of course it may have been stolen."

"Have you checked with the banks?"

"No, chief . . . Ah . . . which bank, sir?"

"How should I know which bank?" But he should know, and he checked the file beside him. "No, she didn't have one, she lived on a small annuity, so if the nephew gets the property he can't expect much cash with it! I have a tracer on him —also similar MOs—be nice if we found a Jacques Frejon in our criminal files under robbery with violence, wouldn't it? As for her, the SP men were asked yesterday to report any sightings of her in the past week, what was she doing, was anyone with her. On that at least we ought to get a good fix— anyone seeing her would have a hard time forgetting! So what are you waiting for? Go ask all the banks if they have perchance an emerald pendant in storage?"

"Right away, chief." But he hesitated. "Just one other thing . . . we had a circular in this morning, about a jewel thief, a young fellow who likes resort areas, we're to keep an eye out for him . . ." He handed the PJ memo to his superior. "Just supposing . . . if there really was an emerald necklace, and she had it under her mattress, and he found out about it . . ."

Jouvet took the flier and read it with interest. "He seduces them first—hum! Well, if he seduced that one, he had a very strong stomach! Still—very interesting, thank you, Sarrazin. See that all the beat men know about this—and if anyone saw someone of this description with our madwoman, we want to hear about it yesterday! *Allez, allez!*"

"Yes, chief." He turned to go. "Ah—and what are you planning to do today? So I won't duplicate . . . ?"

"I," said Jouvet, folding his hands on his belly, "am going to exercise my little gray cells, to see what I may have forgotten. And this afternoon I'm going to report what we're doing to the magistrate, so bring me something to tell him!"

CHAPTER 7

On holiday, a day passes quickly. One has breakfast; one deals with a police commissioner; one lies an hour in the sun letting him drop from one's mind; then it is time to buy the papers and digest them in a relaxed and thorough way—*"Tiens,* skirts this fall will be longer—and an elderly gentleman by the name of Jean Santorini has been knocked down by a car at Saintes . . ." One sips one's coffee slowly, and the air shimmers in immortality; then one decides at last to do a little something—in this case, look at the church at Royan and have lunch there.

Over mussels and omelette, Laura inquired of Marie-Gisèle, "Well, how did you like it, the church?" Modernistic and inventive as it was, she was not sure herself how to appreciate it, and she really wanted to know. "Ah," said Marc, not too busy eating to speak his mind, "it is a glorified pipe organ. And I could not help thinking how much nicer if there was crimson wine, red tomatoes, and yellow leeks for sale behind those glass show window wings!"

Marie-Gisèle looked at him doubtfully. "For shame, Marc! I am sure that in its way it was very impressive . . . I had an old refrigerator once, in just that style!" They all laughed. "But of course"—defensively—"I know nothing about art, I am taking a course in appreciation though at the institute in the fall, and perhaps that will tell me what I should admire about it."

Laura, a little startled by such artificial culturing of culture, hesitated, then decided to probe further: getting to know Marie-Gisèle was part of the holiday, wasn't it? "But how did it make you *feel?* Did you like it?"

She laughed a little, reluctant. "Well, you know I know only what I like . . . and I seem to like, when I go to a church or a museum, only what reminds me of my childhood! At the Orangerie once I fell in love with a painting—I could taste it, feel it, all that clutter of fabrics and flowers and what-nots—it was a Bonnard, I think. Then I realized, that was just as my home was when I was a little girl! Another time, a drift of clouds—my mother had a dress like that, pearly and soft as satin, it must have been one of the first dacrons in France. Or peacock feathers! We had some in a jar, and I still adore peacock feathers, no matter how dreadful! And so you see, all that concrete and glass . . . but," conscientiously, "as the guidebook says, it does soar marvelously."

"When I was a child"—and Marc growled—"a church was cold floors and dank drafts—in fact I thought of God as a perpetual cold in the head."

"Then you ought to like Royan church—air, light"—François was teasing—"and a Joan of Arc in copper—copper saints never sneeze!"

"They never bend, either! Not that I have ever observed such flexibility even on the part of the old carved ones, but at least one can feel that they might—I don't know," he was abruptly nostalgic, "I have lost my innocence, I fear—I do not suppose *le bon Dieu,* if he exists, gives a damn even for Notre Dame; but I imagine that given his choice he would prefer not to be straitjacketed in *béton armé!*"

"If you don't like churches, where are you going to put the churchgoers? They must be accommodated somewhere!" François, in a good mood at the prospect of one thing he could do to counter the exasperation of his ambiguous situation, prepared himself for an amiable and enjoyable wrangle.

"Ah, let them worship under a tree! There at least there is no mistaking the intention of the architect!—But, speaking of nature, *si on allait à la pêche* this afternoon? We can rent a boat, put out our lines, and go into this at our leisure!"

And so, at four o'clock, Laura and Marie-Gisèle found themselves again on the beach and again abandoned. It was too stuffy inside the villa to read or to nap; on the shore blew a light but refreshing breeze; and defended from sun in wide hats and draped towels, Laura read on the blanket while Marie-Gisèle knitted something incredibly complex, fringed with dancing and tangling bobbins. "What are you making?" asked Laura at last, watching her unwind them for the dozenth time. *"Un zhersay argeel,* for the boys. They're all the thing this year, so of course they must have one!"

Laura pondered for quite some time on what a *zhersay argeel* might be before exclaiming, "Oh! A jersey argyll!" Marie-Gisèle giggled. "I can still trick you in French sometimes, Laura—at least, if it's English! Is it hard, always speaking another language? Do you get lonesome for your own?" Laura considered. "No, not really. Not now. At first with Paul . . ." and they were silent a moment contemplating Laura's late husband, spy, sleeper, and would-be assassin of his wife. "But François, you know—" the conclusion was a logical one —"understands well enough, and if the mood takes me, we spend an evening in English."

Marie-Gisèle stole a mischievous glance upward from her knitting needles. "And when you make love—which is it?" "Oh, French, always!"

"You are amusing yourselves, good!" the professor's wife, limping, paused beside them. "May I sit down a moment? I bruised my foot on a stone—I ought to have brought Michel's cane, if I had only foreseen it." "Does he use one, then?" "Oh, as little as possible, but he ought to! Arthritis of the hip . . ." She sat, heavily, laughing. "Men, you know, have their vanities—and so, I suppose, do I—ordinarily I like to keep my arms covered!"

Her legs, long, white, and knobbly, were nevertheless firmly muscled for a woman in her sixties, and Laura exclaimed, "But you are in excellent condition—and you have been swimming."

She nodded. "I adore the ocean—and I play tennis still, when I can, emulate King Gustav—he played, you know, into his eighties! But whatever one does the skin sags—you will see one day when you have the heart of a girl in a body of sixty-eight!"

"One need not," said Marie-Gisèle firmly, knotting two strands together, "be beautiful in order to be attractive, madame."

"Ah merci! I see you have all the makings of a successful flatterer. But call me Germaine—on holidays surely one need not stand on formality—Germaine Moreuil. And what a marvelous thing you are making!"

"Yes, is it not!" Bending over, the journalist's wife cast her shadow upon the jersey argyll and then, without asking, sat cross-legged on the blanket, casting one glance over her shoulder at Jacquot playing along the sea's edge. "Not only policeman's wife, but *tricoteuse* too!" The implication was—unintentionally no doubt—not entirely complimentary, the term *tricoteuse* applying also to those harridans who at the foot of the guillotine knitted while aristocratic heads rolled; and Marie-Gisèle shot her a sharp glance. "You do not knit, madame." And Laura, inwardly applauding the countersuggestion that the journalist's wife did nothing useful at all, intervened with, "Madame Moreuil, are you acquainted with . . ."

"Yvonne Leclerc—But you are at liberty today? Not assisting the police? How goes our little mystère?" The teasing was kittenish, but the kitten had claws.

"I expect," said Marie-Gisèle repressively, "the police have matters well in hand."

"But do they know yet how, or who . . ." It was her husband who wanted to know, no doubt—another scoop for his provincial paper. "The official view is that by night she surprised some thief, and . . ." Mme. Moreuil shivered; it seemed she did not care for the subject either. "Horrible—let us not discuss it."

"Perhaps," said Yvonne Leclerc, not without shrewdness, "it was better than other ways to die. Dramatic, at the very least; and if she was a performer, as your husband said . . ."

"He said nothing of the kind!" Madame Moreuil was unex-

pectedly angry. "It was only a guess . . . that sort of name
. . ."

"Mm . . . But why a thief? Was she wealthy enough to
attract burglars?"

"No, not at all. An annuity . . ."

"But didn't she leave you," she turned to Laura, "an emerald necklace? Or was I not supposed to know that? I forget
who told me, our landlady, or Jean—or was it you, madame?"

Madame Moreuil showed herself even more displeased.
"No, it was not! And I don't see why we must talk about it—
we did not even know her."

"No, but you may have seen her." The more Laura re-
played upon the screen of her memory that little scene before the villa, the more certain she was that Mme. Lemay had
not seen her at all; and under cover of Yvonne's curiosity her
own might pass unnoticed. "Do you remember when Jacquot cut his head, we came up to the villa just as you and your
husband were coming out. And she was there, on the sidewalk, talking to the flower seller. An old lady in most unusual
clothes, almost Edwardian—you could scarcely *not* notice
her!"

Surely Mme. Moreuil paled. "No, indeed, I am sure I would
have remembered."

"Or you, Mme. Leclerc?"

"Oh no!" The disclaimer was hasty. "Well, of course, I had
eyes for nothing but my poor Jacquot—and at such a moment, even if I had seen her, it would have made no impression—certainly not!"

And why was it so obvious she was lying? She frowned after
the two retreating backs. "Now that was curious, wasn't it?"

Marie-Gisèle laughed. "Ah, if you were a policeman's wife,
you would get used to being treated as a cross between a
fortune-teller and a leper!"

François and Marc returned triumphant with one *merlan*
between them, which they triumphantly presented to the
kitchen and which, at dinner, provided three bites of appe-

tizer to the filet de boeuf. Afterward, however, François declared himself not too tired to go out for a cognac, "And I could try at the café to see if Marc's nuns' school exists still—the telephone in Jean's cubbyhole is not exactly the best spot to transact affairs of discretion." So they wandered along the sea front to the bistro where they had drunk morning coffee. François bought his jeton and went off to see what he could discover.

Somewhat to his surprise, the convent did indeed have a listing; and when the number was obtained for him, a brisk young voice answered. He asked for the school's principal, of the Mother Superior. *"C'est moi,* I am head of the school."

"You do not know me, *ma soeur,* but . . ." Having so unexpectedly reached her, the difficulty was where to begin.

"Well?"

"I am a lawyer, from Paris, handling the will of one Annette Frejon, who was once, I think, a pupil at your school."

"Well?"

"That would have been, however, long ago—1906, perhaps as late as 1918 . . . I am searching for her heir, a nephew, but she has left us neither his last name nor his address. And I wondered whether, perhaps, you had any school lists from that time which might establish whether sisters and brothers went to school with her at that time?"

There was a silence, and then the voice, poised on the verge of disbelieving rejection, said, "And *who* did you say you are?"

"François LeBreton, a lawyer. You may call me back, here in Royan, to confirm I exist—or, if you wish, I have Inspector Tavernier here of the Paris Sûreté—he can vouch for my bona fides?" The thing was to throw every possible reference into the barrel and hope that their combined weight might win her conviction. "Inspector Tavernier? And how do I know *he* is what you say he is? Or what does he have to do with this request?"

"My client was murdered, *ma soeur.* And"—he reached for

the last ammunition he had—"she left you a bequest. For the school. For books on the lives of famous actresses."

The indrawn breath betokened a busy exasperation, urgent tasks waiting, total incredulity . . . And then, suddenly, it toppled over into laughter. "Oh naughty, naughty! She begins to interest me, your Annette . . . Frejon? M. LeBreton, I must believe you, you could not have invented this. Now what is it exactly you want me to do?"

"Help me to trace her heir. He will have a carte d'identité, probably, and if his name is Jacques Frejon there will not be too many to sort through in the Dossiers Administratifs; but if he is a sister's son, and she married a man named Dubois? It may take months, and there are some questions of urgency here."

"*Ah oui, je comprends.* Well, M. LeBreton, you are in luck. We are not a proper school now, only a *pouponnière*—but when I moved into this office it was crammed with records going back, I believe, to Napoleon Trois. I had no time to go through them, so I had them removed to the cellar where, no doubt, they are rotting away. But if I have time, I will look— luckily Frejon is not such a common name. And now that I think of it, perhaps—we have a former teacher from that time in the convent here. Soeur Angelique is well over ninety, but her mind is still clear, and her spirit—ah! I will ask her—if Annette Frejon was as mischievous as she sounds, Soeur Angelique may still remember her. But—a, I forget— she was murdered, you say! *la pauvre!*—Yes, on reflection, the murder of one of our former pupils is certainly our affair. You will hear from me soon, *M. l'avocat*—but do not hope for too much!" And, with a last faint echo of laughter, she rang off.

Mopping his brow but glowing with serendipitous pleasure, François returned to their table. "Yes, perhaps, we may learn something! But what an experience, she was terrifying, that young sister. Edith Lemay, I know that you were not quite in your right mind, but you could at least have left me an address book!"

CHAPTER 8

"But that does not make sense! She must surely have had an address book!" Laura sat on the floor the next morning, braiding her hair; the sea air had raised its quotient of unmanageability. And the men had not plotted a straight course after breakfast; they were, by the window of the Taverniers' room, eyeing the weather (variable) and maps (confusing). "But we *can't* get from there to there," Marc said firmly, "this is a seacoast, and even if it doesn't look like it, there's *water* between this road and this."

"François, there must be an address book. Or have been one."

"But there *is* a bridge over the Charente at Rochefort—and a circuit at least on this peninsula." François was stubborn. "There must be others, as well, not shown on the map —roads to little coast villages, to farmhouses . . ."

"Everything in this triangle between us and La Rochelle is a marsh, François—remember your lecture about the sea that went up to Paris? Granted, it is a rather solid marsh, but roads and farmhouses only sit where they can, on the high ground. It's not like traveling from Clichy to Montparnasse."

"Marie, didn't she have an address book?" Laura appealed to the other female, perched on the bed and watching the men with amusement. She now turned her attention to Laura. "An address book? The madwoman? Oh yes, I should certainly think so. Her doctor's telephone number . . ."

"And the name of the place that repairs old furniture . . ." "And her safety deposit box number . . ."

"And the nephew's birthday, plus his children's, if he had any . . ."

"And the woman who made her dresses—they didn't all come from a rummage sale!"

The men stared at them, bewildered: well, of course, men did not have address books. They had secretaries; she was sure Mme. Goulet, François's secretary, had twenty-five years of address books, all date-filed. "Women have address books," Laura explained patiently. "Even if they are old, and write nobody, they have them. How else are they going to remember who recovers cushions, the next time they need them recovered?"

"Or when they are due for the dentist?"

"Or when their last period was? Not that she had any, but I bet she had checkups, at least once a year."

"And if you were old and forgetful, the last thing you'd forget to keep up was your address book—how else would you know what you had to remember?"

"Wait a moment," said Marc, putting the map down. "You are saying there was certainly a record of the nephew's address somewhere—but it may have been taken, or the police just missed it."

They both nodded at him, solemnly, and *"Je t'assure,* Marc!" said Marie-Gisèle.

"If it were there"—François was specific, if doubtful—"do you think you could find it even though the police didn't?"

"Maybe—Oh, I'm sure they looked in the top of her stocking . . ."

"And behind the mantelpiece clock . . ."

"But did they look in the rice jar?"

"Or of course it may have been in an *old* purse, in the little hidden pocket." But neither doubted a moment.

"Well?" François looked at Marc.

"Well, ask Jouvet: *you* ask him, there's no reason why Laura—after all, you're executor! But not right now, ladies, later. Right now we've decided, I think, to go up the coast toward La Rochelle by the shore, and visit one of those beach resorts later if the sun stays out. Agreeable?"

It was agreeable, but meant for Marie-Gisèle a brief scramble to change out of shorts into travel gear . . . Laura, in pants already, wandered to the head of the stairs, thinking of strolling the garden; below, silhouetted against the door, stood two figures who by their eager leaning sway—the negligent drift backward, the curve wristed hand, the open-palmed gesture—were apparently engaged in the age-old game of polite flirtation. Descending halfway, she drew close enough to see features in these shades against the sunshine: Madame Calvet and one of the two handsome young men who had taken a room together. No one had met them, yet; they seemed constantly passing through on the pursuit of pleasure; now Madame Calvet had drawn one into her orbit. They did not hear her approach and looked up startled. "Mme. LeBreton! Do you know M. Machicoulet? My husband is very busy today, writing a speech, and this gentleman has kindly offered to play tennis with me."

Laura took his hand, lightly; it exuded, like Mme. Calvet herself, an intense vigor, a concentrated sexuality. And what kind of a name was Machicoulet? Mâchicoulis, yes. It was, she thought, a kind of barbican, but Machicoulet? He opened the door, gallantly, but she shook her head and they went through it before her, strolling down the walk. As she stood in the doorway Germaine, the professor's wife, passed them and came up the steps, pausing a moment to look over her shoulder. She did not say, "Well!"—her glance said it for her.

And so they drove up to Rochefort on the Charente and walked along the river, and saw Colbert's old arsenal where, in the seventeenth century, he built the newest, most up-to-date fleet France had yet seen. "Forty-seven vessels," said Marc, reading from the guide, "then three hundred built between 1690 and 1800, then the first French naval steamship—it was your English compatriots we were keeping at bay, my dear Laura!"

"And so were we—for the last quarter century of it! I am more interested in the sculpture workshop where they carved prows—and Intendant Bégon, who introduced the begonia to us!" Then there was the obligatory visit to the house of Pierre Loti, with its Arabian room and its memories of his beloved Aziyade: "And why do men insist on falling in love with the exotic, the unattainable?" complained Marie. "If I put on a veil, would you love me more, *mon ami?*"

"Naturally!" said Marc, and ducked her little clenched fist.

"Still," said Laura, "it is very exciting, this sense all along the coast of men and the sea. Han d'Islande—the oyster-culturists and their terrible toil—and think of the arsenal in the days when ten thousand men worked from dawn to dusk, and the sparks flew from the forge, and the hammers were never silent! All that effort, all that energy—and still the sea is almost immune to our technology!"

"Fine," said Marie-Gisèle, "it can keep itself to itself, as far as I'm concerned. Boats make me seasick, and water is very inconvenient—last year when we had that terrible rain, it flooded the cellar and we had neither heat nor electricity for three days. Fortunately, the gas stove . . ." It was clear that Marie-Gisèle held no brief for the sea, and that she would gladly, like King Canute, tell it to stay back—probably armed with a broom to sweep it off if it did not obey her. "But before Rochefort," François wanted to know, "where was the Atlantic fleet built and stationed? At La Rochelle?"

"*Ah, ça existe encore!* Brouage!" François looked at the map over Marc's shoulder. "A little fortified town, almost uninhabited—and right on the coast—we ought to see that!" So they drove along the deserted marshes where once, as Marc reported, immense salt flats had existed until the mud silted them up too. "Now that is a *good* way to make use of the sea," Marie-Gisèle approved, "no labor, no danger—just allow it to occupy your backyard and evaporate into something valuable!"

"Ah!" All four of them were enchanted: Brouage's stone battlements peppered with turrets, covered in thorn and vine with saplings growing out of the towers, rose from the monotonous marsh like some fairy castle sheltering no doubt some *Belle au Bois Dormant* . . . They strolled about the silent village, in and out of archways, along the tops of broken walls, seeing of its four hundred inhabitants only one standing quietly in the doorway of an *épicerie*, two on the terrace of a small restaurant. "One would say a fairy tale!" Marie-Gisèle spoke for all of them. "Oh—and here is the Escalier Mancini!"

Laura's eyebrows rose in surprise. "Ah, you don't know that story! Marie Mancini and Louis XIV—he was only a youth then, and she was niece to Mazarin, and they wanted to marry. Was it a temptation to Mazarin, not only to run France, but to have his niece queen? They must have thought so, to plan at all . . . But you don't make cardinals of such sentimental stuff! He had his heart set on Maria Theresa to cement an alliance with Spain . . . Marie was sent away here, to her uncle the governor, till Louis was safely married off; then she could return to Paris. And Louis *was* married off . . . But on the way back from Spain and the wedding, he ran off from his escort and came here, though she had gone by then, to sleep in *her* bed, walk on *her* ramparts . . ."

"Idiotic!" said Marc. *"Le Lac,* and all that," referring to the poem known to every French schoolboy in which the lake acts as the poet's confidant, reflecting his joy as he boats with his beloved, his solitary grief after her death. But—"I don't see," said Laura frowning, "why she—why they gave up so easily. He was the king, after all!"

"But Mazarin was her uncle—and if he said, 'Go, or you'll enter the convent!'—then!"

"And he was right, after all!" François the lawyer. "The king does not own his own person: he belongs to the state."

"As for her," Marc was cynical, "she had plenty of others to choose from—happily make a grand marriage . . ."

"Ah, but one does not do that!" Marie-Gisèle was incisive. "Eh, Laura? When one has had a chance at the best—the very highest there is—one does not readily descend upon an inferior! For a woman that is her life, her critical moment—

she would do almost anything not to fail there. And if she has failed, lost love and power—ah, the grief can be terrible."

Laura nodded; despite the men's cynicism it was, particularly in this lovely forgotten place, a profoundly moving story. A girl in a black cloak slowly walking the rampart, face averted, eyes dark and tragic; and afterward that other gallant figure, plume in hat, slashed and embroidered doublet, walking the same stones: forever together, forever apart, looking out on the same endless sea.

Driving back through Royan, Marc tossed his head toward Jouvet's office: "Well? You may as well ask him now." Reluctantly François parked, and they all went in with him. "After all, it was our idea, about the address book."

Jouvet's welcome was mixed; she had good legs, Mme. LeBreton, though Mme. Tavernier was more his type, approachable, slightly plump. But lawyers always spelled trouble, and as for the PJ inspector—well, it was not right, even on holiday, that a policeman should lounge about a police office in a flowered shirt! "No, I do not know yet who killed Mme. Lemay," was his greeting.

"No handy villains? No one to shake up?" Marc's sympathy was genuine, and the commissioner warmed to it. "Yes—one —and the Bordeaux Sûreté have shaken him up and found nothing." And that was annoying, for Sonzac had been in Royan on the night in question and, dropping on him unexpectedly, they ought to have found the brooch, the ring . . . still, if he had fenced them already, they would soon find out about it. "And you? What have you to tell me?"

"One small thing." Marc related the incident of the flower seller. "So you see, she saw at least one LeBreton. And we thought, if she had had some alarming encounter—if someone had followed, accosted her . . ."

Jouvet comprehended; yes, thought Marc, a good policeman. "Nothing of that, alas! And we have tried—we have reports of her everywhere, but always on exactly the same route, nothing unusual. Every morning, out of the house, promenade to the end of Pontaillac, back again buying her groceries: every shopkeeper knew her and her two ounces of cheese, her *petite baguette*. Apart from that, she went only to the *Église Protestante* on Sundays and to the weekly concert in Royan. I have talked to the priest, whatever they call him; he is new, he can tell me nothing. To the concert hall I went myself, spoke to the door attendant, who of course knew her: no one had approached her, made her acquaintance, followed her, she arrived and left just as always."

"M. LeBreton"—it would not do to tell Jouvet two women thought his men might have missed something—"would like to know if, at the house, you are finished. He should take inventory, arrange for a caretaker until we have found her heir . . ."

"Oh yes, we are finished!" Jouvet spread his hands wide. "For all the good that it did us, he is welcome to that mare's nest. And as for the heir, we pursue. After all, we know that *he* has a motive, *n'est-ce pas?* though no motive to steal her ring and brooch as far as I can see."

"I have your permission"—François was formal—"to search for him myself, if some useful line occurs to me?"

"Of course, of course, provided you report to me immediately you find him—Ah yes, and I do have one small bit of news to report! We may have discovered your wife's emerald necklace." He grinned, and François was too interested to object that it was not legally in any way his wife's necklace. "You checked with the banks," said Marc.

"We did and found a safety deposit box at the place where she cashed her annuity check. So tomorrow we go with a warrant to open it, if you wish to attend, 10 A.M., *M. l'avocat!*"

CHAPTER 9

Edith Lemay's house was built on the simplest of patterns: two rooms up and two down, the roof cramping the upper story which, in prim resentment, flung out dormers. A Victorian iron fringe outlined the roof peak right, left, and front, and redbrick framing brightened the stone. The yard and the little garden behind were well kept; the madwoman had certainly spent some of her time here. François unlocked the door and Laura stepped gingerly into the hall. "Was this where . . . ?" "Yes." Leading the way to the salon, he looked over his shoulder at Laura. "You will be all right? It isn't . . . ?" "No, of course not!" "If you're not back at the villa by noon, when I'm back from the bank, I'll come and get you." But when he had gone, the little house had a lonely feeling, under the heavy clouds, as if secret messages lurked in its shadows.

"So much the better, then," she said aloud, firmly, and turned the lights on, trying not to feel exposed to some invisible watcher outside. The two rooms, downstairs, were salon and kitchen, but between them, masked from the salon arch by a screen, lay a smaller room off which was the bathroom, inconveniently located downstairs. A glance here showed magazines, plants on the south-facing window, a wicker chair, and a sewing machine, professional, well-used: so much for the idea of the woman who made her clothes for her! Edith Lemay herself had sat here, planning, fingering antique fabrics, and dreaming—of what impossible bygone paradise? She searched the salon first, methodically, but here she expected to find nothing. Dutifully she poked behind sofa cushions, felt the linings of curtains, searched the little desk, where the police had left the papers they had found there. Bills, unpaid and receipted; ancient warranties for iron, radio, carpet sweeper; brochures of Royan's summer season; and one small scrap of paper, torn holes on its inner edge, notated in pencil, "1/2 kg lamb, tomatoes, fennel." Recipe or shopping list?—in any case, Laura kept it. This angular, slightly disorderly writing was her only intimate evidence, so far, of the woman who had lived here.

In the sewing room, she searched thoroughly the box of fabrics, the collection of patterns—where had she found them? some costume agency?—and ran her fingers round the frame of the screen; there was nothing. The bathroom, decrepit and untidy, took longer. Mme. Lemay had not been a spy, to hide waterproof pouch in the toilet tank, but Laura looked anyway. Under the claw-footed bathtub, sweeps of the broom produced nothing but dust fluffs, ancient and large enough for a natural history museum. Towel cupboard, cabinet: threadbare linen, heating pad for arthritis, and a marvelous collection of every kind of cosmetic: for the eyes, for the lips, for the skin, for the hair . . . And no prescriptions save sleeping pills and some aspirin: she had been in good health for her age evidently!

The kitchen presented, at first sight, an insurmountable problem. There was junk everywhere. Cleaning products, scarcely used; dish towels, dishmops; packets of all kinds of food, half empty, stuck in corners, forgotten; unmatching dishes, half sets, glasses, canisters, bonbonnières—cupboards under the sink, and above it too high to reach, in both kitchen and eating area. I will come back, she thought, and clean this room, there is no other way to get at it. But she found herself, even now, putting the kettle on to wash dirty dishes. While it boiled, she ordered the cupboards, sweeping all the junk onto the counters, sponging the shelves, tidying things back again, throwing out half of it, sometimes with nose wrinkling . . . Not a slut, but someone who did not care about food, that was obvious! The glass cupboards with their dishes she left: one could see fairly easily that nothing lay hidden, though she took the tops from tureens to peer in. But to go through every package of sugar, cereal, flour, washing compound—impossible!

It was in the kitchen, nevertheless, that she made her first discovery: upturning the lid of the sugar bowl she saw, folded small and tucked under the lid's inner edge, two thousand-franc notes. The police had missed that: whoever was searching had lifted the lid, stirred about in the bowl, and put the lid back on without inverting it. It was heartening: a little money at least to pay the bills in the salon; heartening that they had missed something left to her to discover; heartening above all that Edith Lemay was a normal woman, hid things in feminine places. "She had a husband, or a man, sometime; that's where one hides money when one thinks he may take what's in one's purse . . ."

The grocery list in her pocket crackled. And that was, perhaps, significant too. Not in the desk nor in the sewing room nor in the kitchen had there been the spiral ring notebook from which that note was torn. It could, of course, be anywhere yet; or she might, in a hurry, have borrowed the scrap of paper. But if she found two such notes and no notebook . . . She took a last look in the kitchen: drawers, counters, windowsill with African violets—it was not there. But Mme. Lemay had loved flowers, growing things; she would water these drooping plants today and warn François that someone . . .

The cellar was empty, so she turned her steps to the second floor. The narrow steep stairs must have been hard for an old lady, and the banister was well worn. Her hand touched the newel post, as Mme. Lemay's must so often have done . . . It was the last thing, perhaps, she had ever touched. Laura shivered.

And, entering the bedroom, paused in shock. A massive jumble—clothes, shoes, on the bed, under it, the bureau cluttered, dusty with spilled cosmetics—and the walls covered with photographs, framed, taped, stuck into one another's corners. Had the police left it like this or found it so and left it not much different? Firmly, she stepped inside. Every shoe, every pocket, each bureau drawer, the large closet—the photos must wait till last, when the rest was disposed of.

Tidily, she handled them one by one, feeling hems, seeking shoe toes. If Edith Lemay had tucked something away for her it would be here—she would not miss it. The bureau drawers, in a jumble, were searched one by one, powder box probed, jewel box upturned and held to the light—but it was empty. So was a small box covered with shells and bearing the legend, "Souvenir of Blackpool," and it ought not to have been. It was in a box just that size and shape that Laura herself kept her old letters.

It was in the closet, in which hung still some voluminous skirts, some blouses with lacy sleeves, that in one gathered sleeve her fingers elicited another crackle. Stick things up your sleeve, of course, in childhood she had done likewise. It was another sheet from the same spiral-ringed tablet: "Write Jacques re will," it said; and the ink was green and fairly recent. Yes; so she did write to Jacques and had had somewhere his address, with safety deposit box number and other memorabilia—perhaps even on the cover of this same notebook, now so curiously missing, and she felt a warm glow of satisfaction with her deductions.

Now for the photographs. They bore, after all, a curious sameness: all these well-made-up faces, these brilliant smiles and twinkling eyes. "Love, Gaby," they said, or "Forever, Harry." The women were all gowned or in costume; the men for the most part in *smoking* jackets; one appeared with violin, another with a seal, ball on nose, another in clown costume. None looked later than the forties. Well, if she had not been a threatrical she had certainly kept theatrical company. Now if I were French and of a certain age, thought Laura, I'm certain I would recognize at least some of them. But she knew no one.

One portrait, professional like the others, caught her eye: a woman's bust, nude from the swell of the breasts up, an incongruous vast velvet hat atop the head: the bold eyes, the strong chin seemed somehow familiar: was this Edith Lemay? That one glimpse had been fleeting, but somehow there was a resemblance . . . Whoever she was, she was handsome; and, hung next to the night table, she would have watched Edith Lemay night and morning.

What was left? only the front bedroom with its dormers, entered from the hall: liberally windowed, yet Edith Lemay had preferred to hide away in the back bedroom. The front room was almost empty; once a sun-room, its wickered chair and table, small cot had not been used for a long age: dust flew up when she touched them. In addition, there was only a tall wardrobe and, in one corner, two suitcases. She opened the wardrobe: empty, except for a shelf on which sat a vast velvet hat—surely the one in the portrait. But dust had grayed its rich blackness and, when she lifted it, what fell out was a mouse nest.

The suitcases—here perhaps were her letters, her other souvenirs of the past—but lifting first one, then the other, she knew at once they were empty. And filthy with dust. Two suitcases, unpacked one day years ago, and left here neglected—yet—only two suitcases? Where was the trunk, the corded box, which must have carried the rest of her possessions? There was no sign of it in the dust, and the cellar had been empty.

Two suitcases. What kind of a woman moved with only two suitcases? Into a new house, a new life, and bringing only the absolute necessities of the past with her? The photographs alone would nearly have filled them—and one could not fit dresses into these narrow cases, certainly not Edwardian dresses like the ones she wore now. Underwear, toothbrush —and the photographs, but if you were leaving your past behind, why bring photographs?

She stepped back into the bedroom and stared at them. They stared back at her, top hats and gowns, all grins and false gaiety, the peculiar brittleness of past triumphs forgotten upon them. And—Edith Lemay had been eighty-three—

almost all must be dead now, only those white grins still glittering in the darkness of the grave . . . Was that why the photographs were here—not as an evocation of past merriment, but as a hairshirt, a memento mori?

CHAPTER 10

They sat about the table in the empty dining room staring at it, the graceful slender snake with its glorious steady green eye glowing in the midst of twinkling diamonds. "But is it real?" Marie-Gisèle, wondering, touched it. "After all, she was mad—and to own such a thing and live on a tiny annuity . . ."

"The annuity was not so tiny when she bought it, I imagine . . . Real? Jouvet thinks so. The bank manager thinks so. But of course it will have to be valued for the estate . . . I assure you, I was nervous about carrying it in my pocket! But I thought, Laura, if we are going to be suspected of murder on its account, you should at least have a chance to see it!"

Marveling, Laura too could not resist touching the slender clasp, the silver-cold arabesques that caught in swirls the diamonds, the arrogant emerald. "I am glad, all the same, it is not mine. Women have been killed for less—and no, Marie, I am not going to try it on. I am not up to it—it demands a king's mistress. But I can see why she kept it—like owning the Mona Lisa—when her others were sold."

The men looked at her in surprise, and she glanced back puzzled. "Well, she had more, of course! No woman owns just one piece of jewelry, and of this quality! Besides, there was the ring, the pin the thief stole. No, she would have sold the rest to buy the house and the annuity."

"Like *La belle Otéro*, naked except for her jewels?" They all understood Marc's allusion to that famed courtesan who at a dinner for intimates had had herself served up on a platter in this costume. "But was there nothing else in her deposit box? No letters, no documents?" Laura was disappointed.

"Only the deed to the house, a bond to cover the other legacies, and her birth certificate. Jouvet now knows the names of her parents, so he may get to the nephew before us." François closed the jewel case, tucked it safe in his pocket. Marie-Gisèle's eyes followed it, and she sighed, "But perhaps Laura has found something?" Her own sex, her tone implied, was also capable of detection.

Laura, recalled to her morning's activities, laid four pieces of paper on the table. "Two thousand-franc notes to add to the estate, chéri—found tucked in the lid of the sugar bowl. And"—she touched the other scraps—"I am now sure there was an address book."

Marc picked them up curiously. "Yes, of course this is significant. If she was writing to the nephew his address was somewhere. But a half kilogram of lamb? Perforated edges? These are not leaves from an address book!"

"No, it's a reminder book—disposable."

Marie-Gisèle exclaimed, "Of course! I also have two. One, with the addresses, I keep in my purse; the other is in the kitchen for jotting down what I need to buy, appointments and so on; and when I have done whatever it is, I tear out the leaf. But you didn't find the book it belonged to!"

"Neither that nor the address book, if there was one. If she had only a few things to remember, they might have been on the back cover of this book."

Marc frowned. "It is suggestive—but it is not evidence. Now if something more substantial could be shown to be missing . . ."

Laura hesitated. "I don't know, but . . ." She described the letter-sized shell box, empty, and the bedroom's disorder. "I just wonder, Marc, if Jouvet didn't jump to conclusions too readily. The kitchen was in total disorder, I agree, but the salon was neat enough, and who leaves her lovely dresses all over the bed? It's not even practical—you'd have to move them to sleep, surely?" Marie-Gisèle nodded vigorously.

"You think then"—François was interested—"that someone searched the whole house, and not just for valuables? But the shell box might have had jewelry too, you know!"

"Like the jewel box next to it? Oh, maybe—but one does not search closets for jewels."

"If you knew her a madwoman you might." Marc was sardonic.

"Was she mad? Not in the ordinary sense, I think. I had the impression . . ." She described the bedroom, its photographs, the black velvet hat, the two suitcases. "It told, perhaps, a story. She was in the theater, at least till the war . . . then, or sometime later, something happened. Some sort of . . . moral reversal? She goes to church each week, Jean tells us she disapproved of beach nudity—yet thirty years before she had been performing in almost nothing but a black velvet hat . . . does that sound to you like the same person? Anyway . . . at that point she sold all she had, bought an annuity, and moved here, cutting herself off; and though I can't guess why, began to wear dresses in the fashion of her childhood . . . And here she stayed for twenty years and more until someone killed her."

Marc listened, seriously. "You are suggesting it was no mere thief—that someone returned from the past, killed her, and searched the house to remove any trace of the connection . . ." He shook his head, slowly. "It doesn't wash, you know."

"Why not?"

"Because to kill her like that—if it was not a thief in a panic it was someone who hated her. And one does not hate enough to kill for twenty years, it is not in human nature."

Reluctantly, Laura conceded; François and Marie-Gisèle too saw his point. "All the same, when you go to the station, will you ask Jouvet about the clothes on the bed and the notebook? Perhaps his men put the clothes there, searching . . . perhaps without thinking, someone stuck the notebook in a pocket."

"Oh, we shall all go—give François a bodyguard for his treasure. But even if Jouvet believes you about the notebook and the searcher, Laura, you won't catch him looking for a murderer of a generation ago!"

As they moved out into the hall, Jean Calvet came down the stairs, looked at them, turned, and looked back again hesitating. "I wonder if you have seen my wife?" They shook their heads.

"She was supposed to be back by now—but perhaps she's come and gone out again." He stood on one foot, wandered toward the door; past him, in the salon, sitting next to her husband, Germaine Moreuil cast Laura a significant glance.

So once more they drove to Jouvet's office; François knew the way now, down the Avenue de Pontaillac to the Avenue de Cordouan to the square by the strange concrete cathedral; and, as they parked and crossed the street, Marc observed, "If we arrive at this time one more day, Jouvet will call for le four o'clock every time he sees us." But Jouvet was not there; Sarrazin, who invited them into his office, explained, "He's off early today—he attends a soccer banquet this evening for our triumphant team, of which his third son is a member, so he rests up for this important occasion."

"See," said Marc to François, "what is in store for you!" and François to Marc, "Even sooner for you, and doubled!" To Sarrazin, "Will you take charge of this necklace, then, and put it in the police safe for us?"

"Surely." Sarrazin was more than agreeable. "And what has Madame found, visiting the house of the crime this morning?—Ah yes, our beat man is alert, you see!"

Such amiability was not to be wasted; she told him about notebook and box and asked about the dresses. "No, I inquired about that too, before the bedroom was photographed. But that was just how it was, all the dresses in a heap on the bedclothes. That proves nothing, of course. We saw the empty box and supposed he had taken its contents and that may apply to the wardrobe too—he flung the clothes out to search the shelves. Your little notes, I agree, are interesting, but they leave us nothing to pursue, do they? If the intruder took them to remain anonymous, he has effectively succeeded! No," and he slid off the corner of Jouvet's desk on which he had irreverently been sitting, "what puzzles me is the *way* she died."

François raised an eyebrow, and Marc nodded encouraging. "Envision then—here is Mme. Lemay, standing in the doorway." He placed himself in the doorway of the office. "Is it not a protected place to be? Safe in the rear, and guarded on both sides by the doorjamb. In front of her stands . . . myself." And shifting about, he became now the assassin. "I carry a curved narrow wooden object of some sort, which she apparently does not find threatening—but if she does, she has only to scream, put her arms up, shut the door. Eh?"

"Right." Marc was professionally interested.

"Instead, what happens? She turns sidewise, as if to allow the person to enter—distinctly odd, if this is a stranger with an obvious weapon—and I? What do I do? I could follow her in, kill her out of sight of the street, or simply strike the back of her head when it is turned to me. Instead I raise my . . . piano leg . . ."

"Billy club . . ." Marc.

"Cricket bat?" Laura.

"And swing *through* the doorway with its narrow jambs, being lucky enough to catch her on the temple. That is how it happened, no doubt about it. And I go over and over it in my head, but it still does not make sense."

"Unless," said Marc slowly, "the weapon . . ."

But Laura found this reenactment unbearably distressing. "Have you talked to the flower seller? Had he anything . . . ?"

"Yes, madame, and he says she said only, '*Mon Dieu*,' once and asked him to call a taxi. Are you going to dinner next? There is a nice little place, just off the Grande Conche, which . . ."

They accepted his advice and, as the place had a public telephone, François departed as soon as they had ordered. "That nun—she will have nothing yet, I suppose, but at least I can ask . . ." Laura, out of cigarettes and seeing a Tabac sign next door, went out to buy them and returning, observed the journalist and his wife, heads together, at one of the sidewalk tables. They had not seen her, and she paused a moment: they were, as usual, in disagreement about something. *"Mais c'est fou!"* she was saying, aghast, and he, "What do you expect? After all, we need the money!" They were almost a comedy act, she thought, always to one side of the stage, always quarreling and always inscrutably, Beckett fashion: "What about my uncle's old muffler?" "And what about the pen of my aunt?" Perhaps it was their habitual enjoyment— after all people did enjoy Beckett!

François's hors d'oeuvres were cold, fortunately, for he took a long time to return, looking, for a lawyer, remarkably pleased. "She has it! At any rate, she has something, for as far as that takes us!" He started to eat voraciously.

"Tiens!" said Marc, and they waited, leaning anxiously toward him, until he had finished. "Well! There was a sister, and only a sister, no other Frejons in the record. She talked to the old nun first, which speeded up things remarkably . . ." ("I told you," she had said in her amused reproving young voice, "Soeur Angelique is a marvel.")

"She remembered the girl? Our Edith-Annette?"

"Oh, very well—an imp of mischief, I should imagine! The father was a watch repairer and a jeweler in a small way . . ."

"Ah!" Marie-Gisèle approved. "Then in the way of jewelry she would know what she was getting."

"And the sister, two years older, was it appears very talented. At any rate, they had a visitor one day from Paris who was much struck by her art notebooks and, in particular, the sketches of ladies in ball gowns with which she had adorned the margins. So much so that when the visitor returned, she got for Elise Frejon a position as apprentice in one of the big fashion houses of Paris."

"That, of course, is why Soeur Angelique remembers—it must have been quite an event in convent school history!" Laura was satisfied.

"Distinctly memorable, one would imagine! It was so spectacular a chance, at any rate, that the whole family moved to Paris. The mother—she was Protestant, Soeur Angelique remembers—wanted to keep an eye on her daughter, and the father's business was small enough so that he could transport it easily."

"And Annette?"

"Went too, of course, and later took to the stage, one supposes." He had asked Soeur Richarde what she intended to do with the legacy. "We shall buy copies of Racine's sacred play *Esther* for the church library and a biography of its sponsor Madame de Maintenon to go with it, to show our girls that even a king's mistress can achieve piety. This will, I think, fulfill the letter of the bequest if not the spirit?" He chuckled, remembering.

"She must have stayed on in Paris, the sister."

"Yes, and became one of the chief cutters of the House of . . ." He spoke a name still eminent in the annals of fashion: there was a stir of interest among the women.

"Did she!" Marc sat back, intrigued. "You know, there might be a line to follow there—she would be dead now, of course, but houses like that have their own traditions—not like the Prisunic! Someone might well remember her and, if she married, the name of her husband . . ."

"Ah! But if you think I am going to Paris to ask questions, in the midst of my holiday . . ."

"No, but . . ." He had suggested this chase in the first place to distract François from the irritation of his own position, but there was more to it now. From the beginning, and especially since he had listened to Laura and Sarrazin this morning, doubts had stirred murkily. "I have the feeling it might be wise for us to talk to this nephew as soon as possible, and the questions we want to ask might not be the same as Jouvet's at all."

"What sort of person she was—her past history—" Laura nodded. "Robert might do it!"

"Of course!" Marie-Gisèle's assent was vigorous. François's

uncle by marriage and foster-father was as curious as a cat, and his impulsive eccentricities had lured more than one unwary stranger to consider his curiosity harmless. "He goes up to Paris regularly to the Affaires Culturelles, it would give him an entrée . . ."

"And if you call him I can talk to Franchot!" Franchot was not yet, of course, old enough to talk, and the arrangement had been that Robert and Solange would call them only if there was cause for concern, but she was suddenly lonesome for baby noises. Reluctantly, François went back to the telephone, Laura eagerly at his side; and after the customary formalities had been exchanged with Montargis and Laura had heard one glorious crow from Franchot at the sound of her voice, François asked for Robert. "Would you like to ask a question or two for us in Paris, Papa Rob? Explore in the world of fashion?"

Robert was only too happy. "I can see my grandson in the evenings only, and Solange insists he must be in bed by seven —what do you think of that! Grandfathers I thought had special privileges!" He was indignant. "What am I to find out?"

François explained, and Robert took his notes, then hummed a bit. "But what do you want to know this for? Are you into mischief again? I thought you were on holiday!" Reprobation. "So we are, Papa, but . . ." Laura took the receiver. "It is like this, Papa Rob . . ." and she explained succinctly what had happened in Pontaillac. When she had finished there was a moment's silence. *"Quoi! Ladite Edith!* Who would have thought it!—I think," he said in sudden decision, "I had better come see you." "Go to Paris first!" But he had hung up while she was speaking.

"He knew her—yes, I am sure of it!" she answered François's questioning glance. "And when he comes he will explain everything . . . Oh, François, isn't it splendid?" She flung her arms about her husband; not until this moment had she realized how deeply she had been concerned for him.

CHAPTER 11

And then, after all, it seemed there would be no need to unearth the past—the newspapers would do it for them. *Le Monde,* the next morning, had the news on an inside page, and the less conservative papers would certainly soon have more.

The *Le Monde* story was brief, with no photograph, but for provincial news that was good coverage. "A correspondent in Royan informs us that the old woman murdered four days ago, and named in police reports as Annette Frejon, was in fact Edith Lemay, well-known star of the cabaret and the music hall in the years between the two wars.

"Mlle. Lemay began her career as singer and dancer with the C. B. Cochran troupe in England during the First World War. She appeared in revues at the Casino de Paris and the Olympia with Mistinguett and Chevalier, but our readers will remember her best as The Girl in the Black Velvet Hat and as the star of the revue, Vingt Ans de Music-Hall, which enjoyed great success in the spring of 1939 until the outbreak of hostilities closed the theater season.

"Of late years it appears she had lived retired in Royan following a period as instructress in vocal and dance arts.

"Mlle. Lemay was killed on the night of the —th in her home, and her body was discovered next day by the postman.

"The Sûreté Urbaine at Royan, which is handling the case, is treating it as an affair of robbery with violence."

"There!" said Marie-Gisèle, who had been looking over Marc's shoulder as he read aloud. "It is just as the professor said—she was on the music halls."

"He did not say exactly that—" Laura recalled, "he said the name was theatrical."

"Well, but the two other names he mentioned were music hall, I am sure of it!"

"The Girl in the Black Velvet Hat . . ." Laura remembered a photograph, a black velvet hat with a mouse nest . . .

They were, once again, at the little café near the beach which they seemed to have adopted: this morning Laura had declared herself famished and, after eating the villa's continental breakfast, demanded an American one. The Taverniers, watching her eat, had formed their own conclusions as to what exercises had produced such an appetite. Now she pushed back her plate and said vigorously, "But now, you see, we are getting somewhere. Between what the papers will dig up and what Robert can tell us, perhaps Jouvet will stop suspecting François!"

Once again Marc demurred. "It is not suspicion exactly; he just wants him explained." "And I!" François let out a long breath. "*I* want myself explained. In fact, I have seldom felt myself so inexplicable as during the past few days! Now, at least, perhaps we can get on with our holiday."

"Yes!" Marie-Gisèle was as vigorous. "What about these Romanesque churches? For six months I have been menaced with Romanesque churches and I have not seen one yet!"

Marc groaned. "But the sun is out!"

"Very well, we shall swim this morning, but this afternoon we shall drive to Saintes. In a town with a name like that, there *must* be Romanesque churches."

Then they had to discuss whether or not to swim at another *conche,* as the locals called those deepening crescents of sand between headlands which made the region so attractive a beach resort; but François, who did not like wearing a bathing suit under pants or changing in bushes, voted for Pontaillac. So it was that when Laura, hungry again, went to the beach stand for an ice, she joggled the elbow of Germaine Moreuil, well covered today in white ducks and a sun visor.

She brushed Laura's apologies aside energetically. "No, it was my fault, I was watching the Calvets."

"Where?"

"Strolling the sand, there. They are almost a royal couple, you know, Jean and Jeanne. He nods to the unheard plaudits, almost imperceptibly, and she walks beside, silent, impervious . . ."

"He found her yesterday?"

"Yes, she came back saying she had an errand—but she was with that young man Gilbert, you know. I saw them laughing together at the beach hut . . . I should not gossip, I know," she was apologetic, "but it is my hobby—I am interested in people."

"I scarcely know him, only by name, and his friend not at all."

"Nor I—but the friend has not been so lucky as Gilbert, I think! Michel and I went last night to a harbor café where there is good jazz, and he was there with an older woman—a divorcée, I suppose, in her early forties, with a *very* deep cleavage."

Laura envisioned her at once, heavily tanned, beringed, one of those who removed their bikini bras on the beach knowing that the body stays young longer than the face. They began to stroll back together in a mutual liking. "Oh, you can tell your husband he is quite right, Edith Lemay was indeed on the music halls."

"Oh?" She stopped.

"Yes, *Le Monde* has a story this morning."

"*Vrai?* Yes, you are quite right; I must tell him that." She shook hands, firmly, and stumped off across the sands at a pace remarkable for a woman in her late sixties.

And so they drove to Saintes: a snug little city on a curve of the Charente which seemed to say, "If you locate in a snug little spot on the curve of the Charente with some good land and fish in the river, on the pilgrim route to St. James of Compostela, you can very comfortably survive the Romans, and the Middle Ages, and the Wars of Religion, and even the

Age of the Atom." In the old city, following a neatly chronological route, they visited first the Roman arena (convenient to a parking lot), its grassy tiers untrodden now by the onetime twenty thousand watchers of Roman spectacle; and then penetrated through streets of handsome classical hotels to St. Eutrope and St. Pierre.

Marie-Gisèle was offended by St. Eutrope, half of whose vast bulk had been removed to allow traffic to circulate in the center city. "Only a choir and a crypt . . . and the steeple looks far too big for the church," she complained. "Well, but after five centuries things do tend to fall apart," Marc teased her, "and—businessmen are the only pilgrims nowadays, you see!" As for St. Pierre, she observed faithfully the tower from which the Angelus was first rung, the spot where the inventor of the guillotine was born, and the Gothic nave rebuilt after the Protestants vandalized it in 1568, but remained unsatisfied. "This is Gothic, isn't it? Pointed arch Gothic, round Romanesque? How am I to know Romanesque churches if you will not show me a complete and proper one?"

It was a valid complaint and, hopefully, they crossed the river past Germanicus's arch to the Abbaye aux Dames. "Ah, here! Now that is surely Romanesque, isn't it?" Tranquil of facade, solid, unbuttressed, its squat open-arched towers topped by gently bulging fish-scaled cones, it did not soar but sat serenely, warm, plump, and comfortable as a hen gone broody. "Now I shall know—they are quite different, aren't they? Little chapels popping out of the choir, and that flat arcading like cake decoration! I can see one could develop a taste for it—but why is it called the Ladies' Abbey?"

"Because it was an abbey of aristocratic nuns, and they had a school here for girls of good family." Laura was reading the guidebook. "And—look, Marie—Mme. de Montespan was a pupil here! Athénaïs de Rochechouart, future marquise de Montespan! A lovely name, Athénaïs; if I had a girl, do you think . . ."

Marie-Gisèle shook her head dubiously. "The associations

might not just be . . . but isn't it curious how we keep running into Louis XIV's mistresses! Were the girls prettier here?
No, it can't be that, Marie de Mancini didn't come from the
west . . . What do you suppose she thought about, the
young Athénaïs, sitting over her books? Would she ever have
guessed that . . ." And they thought, for a moment, of that
beautiful woman who bore Louis seven children and saw
them all carried off at birth to be raised by others, most
notably Mme. de Maintenon, who in the end supplanted her.
François found himself reflecting upon Soeur Richarde's proposed use of her legacy and wondering whether it met the
letter of Edith Lemay's wishes . . . Well, Mme. de Maintenon had commissioned two classic French plays and wasn't
her first husband the crippled Scarron, a dramatist who had
even written a play about strolling players?

They got back late and tired and ate at the villa, finishing
somewhat after the other diners; and when they retired to
the salon for coffee they found almost everyone there. The
Calvets, in two deep chairs by the window, each reading a
paper and resembling a senior and junior board of directors;
Gilbert Machicoulet and his friend sipping brandy at a small
table and murmuring in some secret laughter; the professor
and Germaine by the fireplace at chess, he popping his pieces
out triumphantly, she more thoughtfully. But their table for
four was still empty: the Italian family knew enough not to
inflict their children on the after-dinner serenity.

"Well! And where have you been today?" The professor
turned to them, his white beard waggling cheerfully. "To
Saintes! Ah, Saintes of the pilgrim route! Do you know, I have
often speculated on whether these routes are not far older
than the Middle Ages, older than Christianity: the English
still have their old trackways, I believe, and one goes to
Canterbury . . ." He was well away, and Marc said quietly to
François, "I'm going, while they are all here, to make a phone
call."

"We found something else interesting at Saintes," Marie-

Gisèle confided to Germaine, "did you know Mme. de Montespan went to school there?"

"Did she! I wonder what it was like, teaching those girls, and knowing yourself the temptations they would be exposed to. It must have been difficult, teaching fidelity to a husband, knowing he would be chosen for them, almost certainly be unfaithful . . . Yet you could scarcely, given your profession, say 'Do the best you can, and if you can't be good be careful' "

"If indeed," Marie-Gisèle said sagely, "any of them were willing to listen!" Gilbert's companion looked up, amused. "Wasn't it Mme. de Montespan who was involved in the poisons' affair—sent her maid to black masses to get Louis back for her? A fine end to a convent education!"

"One wonders"—Gilbert tapped off his cigarette ash—"or I did, in school, just what was the point of taking away all those bastards to be raised elsewhere. Secrecy? But surely M. le marquis de Montespan was not an idiot—he must have noticed something! Or did Louis just tap him on the shoulder and say, "Stay away from your wife for the next nine months, my boy!"

They snickered, not entirely agreeably, and Jean Calvet lowered his paper decisively. "Mme. de Montespan was not only a lovely woman, but a brilliant one—an entirely fitting consort for Louis had politics allowed it. And one could scarcely expect him, attractive, able, at the height of his powers, to content himself with a totally incompatible Maria Teresa."

"It is Mme. de Maintenon I detest!" Mme. Calvet's interjection was unexpected. "Sneaking about, playing mama to everyone, acting the prude, stealing Louis behind her back— and the Revocation of the Edict of Nantes was the only good thing she ever accomplished!"

Her husband emitted a strangled murmur, and the professor said, "Come now—I can't accept that—my mother was a Protestant!"

Mme. Calvet looked at him in genuine surprise. "Oh no—I

didn't mean—I meant all that false prudery, and when she really did something honest about her convictions, it was a disaster!" And her bitterness was convincing.

"What have you learned?" François asked sotto voce as Marc slid back into his seat. Marc's eyes narrowed in anticipation. "I called *Le Monde* about the story—they got it from a newspaperman who happens to be on holiday here. And his name, my friend, was Jacques Leclerc—now what do you make of that one?"

CHAPTER 12

Laura rose early next morning, a yearning upon her to walk that smooth silver-rimmed beach before another foot touched it. François, hair tousled upon the pillow, slept still, curled in the hedgehog question mark of the imperious defensive spirit, and she looked down on him tenderly. The apartness of another is capturable only unawares and, so caught, is instantly loved both for the unawareness and the apartness: a love with a bittersweet poignancy. Well, if she left him now, it would be only to return with a sharper savor . . .

But, at the head of the stairs, she was obstacled by young Jacquot Leclerc, soundlessly bouncing his ball from one carpeted step to the next, catching and reaiming in the same deft gesture. Looking up, he lost rhythm, and the ball bounded away to stop at the front door. Chasing it, he made room for her and politely held the door open. Bending down she said, nevertheless, "You ought not to block the stairway, Jacquot; people need to use it."

"Oh, I know." His air was jaunty, precocious. "That's why I got up early, we're going tomorrow, you see, and when we came I thought I would try my ball on the stairs—you have to hit every step, you see, not miss any, and not drop it!"

"So you're leaving tomorrow!"

"Yes, we came for a week, and it's nearly over, and I have *so many* things to do yet!" He looked injured, she touched his shoulder and went out but he followed her to the steps, hesitant. "One thing I would like to do . . . can I see your emerald necklace?" She was taken aback. "Ought I not to have asked? I'm sorry, Mother said you had an emerald neck-lace and"—he was wistful—"I've never seen a real emerald."

"I'm sorry, Jacquot, I don't have it. It's not really mine, you see; it belonged to an old lady and it will go to her heirs."

"I know." He nodded decisively. *"La Folle.* She was mur-dered you know. And I saw her, that day we came up from the beach. And then, later on, I heard her talk, too!"

"You did? How did that happen?"

"Oh . . ." He was pleased with the importance her sud-den attention gave him. "It was after lunch, my head ached, and Mother said I was impossible, always fussing. So Jean said I could come with him in the little room there by the front door, you know, where the desk is and the telephone. He said he would show me a shark's tooth."

"And she came there?"

"No, Jean said I could answer the telephone and say 'Villa Brise de Mer,' like he does, so when it rang this lady said this is May something and I want Jean. I told him and he said, 'Oh, *La Folle!'* not wanting to talk, I guess. But I did hear her."

"And what did she say to Jean? Do you know, Jacquot?"

He looked vague. "I dunno," and went back in the door-way. "Oh—it was something about who was staying? I *did* see the shark's tooth, and do you know, it can cut paper?"

Marc, coming down to a fresh croissant and a solitary Fran-çois, said, "What are we doing today? Do you think Robert is likely to turn up yet?"

François looked up, buttering. "I was wondering the same thing. You will want to tell Jouvet what you found out . . . and if Robert went to Paris, there is no way to get in touch with him. Badly arranged, the whole thing!"

Laura, arriving, heard him and sat down with a neat tuck to her skirt. "Well but," she pointed out, "it was not my doing. He rang off before I had a chance to say more. Where is Marie-Gisèle this morning? Sound asleep?"

"No, lazing about," but at that moment she appeared in the doorway, refreshed and indolent. "Oh, what a marvelous

day! Pour me coffee, *chéri!* And what are we going to do with
it?"

"Let us," François proposed, "do nothing. Swimming, and
mussels at that place by the beach for lunch, and if by then
we are bored, we can see what offers: a concert, a fête, a drive
along the Gironde shore."

So they offered themselves to the sun; but scarcely had
they disposed themselves on the beach rug and admired the
sea with one peaked sail on the horizon than Jean came
running across the sand. "M. LeBreton, he has telephoned,
your father, he is waiting for you!"

Robert's voice on the telephone was casual, but rich in self-
satisfaction. "Yes, I have found your nephew for you . . . I
hoped to catch you earlier at breakfast, but there was still one
person to see. I shall now take the train to Royan—I am in the
station—and arrive about 6 P.M. if you can meet me?"

"Of course, Papa Rob—but who is he, this nephew?"

Robert sounded miffed. "In a moment, yes—I have it here
on a slip of paper—are you not pleased I have been so prompt
and, if I say so myself, so ingenious? And you will owe me the
rail fare, naturally?"

"Naturally! And naturally, I am profoundly impressed! But
who is he?"

A pause: Robert was putting his glasses on. "He lives in
Marseille, and his name is—um—journalist by profession, too!
—Jacques Leclerc."

"Jacques Leclerc!" The emergency meeting in the
Taverniers' room followed instantly, and Laura was
reproaching herself. "Of course, I might have guessed—every time I heard them talking it was something about *folle* or
fou—only I kept hearing Jacquot as Jacko!"

"We must"—Marc ignored this linguistic byway—"notify
Jouvet."

"People we know!" Marie-Gisèle was not happy. "How
disagreeable!"

"Yes, but you must tell Jouvet right away: they are leaving

tomorrow." Not inquiring how she knew, Marc decided, "I had better not phone from here—if someone heard, then . . . The café. But *not* in our bathing suits. Or would you prefer to, François?"

"No, better you. You know, if it is this fellow, and he did . . . With no other heirs, no residuary legatee, it is going to be extremely awkward!"

They stayed on at the café for an aperitif; they had no wish to be at the villa when Jouvet arrived. And not one but felt vaguely guilty. "That poor little boy!" mourned Marie-Gisèle. *"Va pour sa mère,* but he at least has done nothing!"

"Well, we do not know that Leclerc has!" Marc was cross.

"Oh, voyons, mon cher! If he were innocent, he would at once have come forward. If it were *your* aunt, at the very least you would have inquired!" Marc said gloomily that in this case it was Jouvet who had inquired for *him,* and he had promised to be at the station at four . . . So, fleeing the whole situation, they drove out along the coast, blind to the scenery, to take an inferior lunch with no mussels, in a far from holiday mood. "And she telephoned Jean to make sure it was they?" Laura wondered. "But she never saw *him*— would she have recognized the other two? And if so, why would that shock her?" It was all vaguely unsatisfactory.

Jouvet leaned back, hands on the arms of his chair, which groaned. "He says he had no idea he was her heir, and he is lying. He says he didn't kill her, and he may be telling the truth. He says he didn't report his presence because he didn't want his holiday to be spoiled by police questioning!"

Marc laughed. "That is stupid enough to be true! Has his room been searched? Has he an alibi?"

"Only his wife—and she—she would say anything, that one. Do you know, she called me a Nazi?" He was deeply offended. "And we still have our other candidate, a real *voyou,* perfectly capable of it. The trouble is, there is no hard evidence. The ring, the pin. We have circulated descriptions, but what is to stop whoever it is from hiding them indefinitely, or throwing them into the Gironde? The weapon. Nothing in the Leclerc room . . . nothing anywhere that we can get our hands on . . . Tell me, *mon ami*, you thought from the beginning this was a personal crime."

Marc shrugged. "You know your territory far better than I do—but she let him into the house."

"Yes, and then he stepped over her body and proceeded to search the premises—removing, Sarrazin suggests to me, anything with his name on it? But a real thief would have done the same, and a real thief would have no trouble inventing a tale to win the confidence of a madwoman . . . And whatever we presume, we have the same contradiction: a cool thief, and a panicky killer."

"Striking in an odd posture, with an odd weapon—yes, I have been listening to Sarrazin too! Couldn't the lab be more precise about it?"

"An object about one inch in width, with rounded edges, and a slight curve to it. Length unknown, of course, but if it had been excessively long he could not have wielded it through the doorway. It could have been anything . . . the leg of your chair." This, of bentwood, splayed its rear supports slightly, and Marc glanced down at it uncomfortably. "It could also have been—a slat from a park bench, a crowbar, a child's sailboat!" he noted.

"I know . . . I find myself wandering about my wife's kitchen, touching: was it this? was it this? There are so many objects in the world today, and you can kill an old woman with most of them if you are determined upon it! I remember a case Sarrazin handled, some years ago—wife dead, beaten around the head, no alibi for the husband. He was in the shed fixing a toy, he said, and the neighbors had seen him there; and no weapon! Finally Sarrazin got around to asking him exactly what he was fixing: it was his kid's tricycle, and the handlebars . . . He had them off, went in to speak to her, didn't like what she said, gave her a few cracks on the head, went out, and screwed them back on again!"

"But doesn't the lab know whether it was iron or wood, or what it was made of?"

"No, only one thing, that it was wrapped in plastic-coated cloth—a purchase used as a weapon on an impulse? Or so that she wouldn't see? But they found flecks of gray plastic, a thread or two . . . a shopping bag, that's my guess."

"The devil! The things we have to deal with! And now the press too, I suppose."

"Oh yes." Jouvet was gloomy. "I can see them—famous artiste's nephew questioned—journalist harassed by police—a neat little case, and now it goes slopping over in all directions! I am a stupid old man, *mon cher,* and I shall be happy for anything you happen to pick up around the villa—especially if it is an old chair leg with specks of gray plastic!"

Marc laughed; his opinion of Jouvet's abilities was far higher than that, and he bore no grudge at having been held at arms' length up till the present. "You are an old shark! but if I can be your pilot fish I shall do my best. I suppose you told Leclerc to keep himself available?"

"Oh yes: the examining magistrate wants to see him tomorrow! His holiday will be prolonged willy-nilly."

"Pauvre type! I wonder if he can afford it?"

"Well, if he can't, your lawyer friend will just have to advance him the money!"

"He can't very well do that—if he murdered her!"

"Then at the worst he has only to confess, and we will be happy to provide accommodations!" And he grinned his old shark's grin.

CHAPTER 13

Robert, beard jaunty, a *Paris Soir* under his arm, descended from the evening train. He was a small man, quicksilver by nature, and staggered a little under Laura's impetuous hug. "Yes, yes, your infant is well; if you examine my jacket closely you will see teddy bear hairs. Ah, François, and what mischief have you gotten yourself into now? *La belle Edith*—hum! the sins of the fathers!" He grinned wickedly. "But no, I cannot say another word until I have eaten—I have forgone my lunch for you!"

It was sheer provocation, but it was not in his nature to remain silent for long; only, over oysters in the best restaurant in Royan, he demanded to know first what exactly had happened. Marc was spokesman and, his tale peppered by Robert's *Ahs* and *Tiens!*, he recounted the progress of the case to date—including specific details about the weapon wrapped in gray plastic.

"Depend upon it," said Robert dogmatically, "it will turn out to be something very simple. Part of a playpen, perhaps: reconstructing the one which you brought, Laura, is certainly a fatal adventure!"

"It makes one think," said Marie-Gisèle reflectively, "how easy it is to kill someone . . . My heavy fondue pot, Marc, if I stuck that in a plastic bag, demolished you with it, and dropped the bag in the Seine—back on the shelf there would not even be a mark on that pot, I assure you!"

"*Merci,*" said Marc. "When I find you purchasing a strong shopping bag, I shall take my precautions."

"But it would have to be heavy, surely"—François was curious—"if it cracked someone's skull?"

"Not necessarily"—Marc's middle name was prudence—"it would depend a great deal on the strength of the attacker—his leverage—and of course she was an old lady, bones brittle."

Robert grieved, head bent, over his asparagus. "An old lady! it is hard to believe that . . . so lovely . . . No, no, not until after coffee and Armagnac!"

It came, and François, who knew his man well, said firmly, "Bargain complete, Papa Rob—now for your researches!"

Robert tested the Armagnac with approval, sat back, beamed on them, and began. "Well, then. I went to the Maison in Paris to which you directed me, and a hard time I had of it! The fall collections, it seems, are in full preparation, and even the President of France is not allowed an advance look at them. Without my credentials from the ministry, I could not have set foot in the door, and even promising them a state film for export barely got me into the workshops! It was there, I thought, I might find an old employee or so—the direction is now in the hands of a younger generation, of course."

"And so . . ."

"I penetrated at last to the depths of the establishment. Depths indeed! The confusion, the untidiness, scraps of fabric, pins everywhere. They scurry about with bits of dresses as if they were secret messages, and one sees models, bare in the most unexpected places, sauntering through constantly—one scarcely dares look!" His beard bristled, affronted; of course he had enjoyed it immensely, but the real offense was that they had not looked at him. No more attention than if he had been somebody's poodle! in fact, a great deal less, for one of the models had on a string a stray kitten which no one neglected to pet.

"Well?"

"Well then . . . I was given a discourse on the fashion trade, paused here and probed there—and by one little lady with a mouthful of pins draping some sort of shiny stuff on a statue I lingered sometime: she informed me it was moire taffeta she was draping, and not on a statue but a dressmaker's dummy. So—'Did you know Elise Frejon, who worked here a long time ago?' I said, and she took all the pins out. 'Elise Frejon, fancy anyone who remembered.' Of course"—he preened—"she had known her, had learned her trade from her. Elise Frejon was a cutter. Did you know, that is very important, a cutter? You work from the designer's drawings, but you also are a creator: you see at once how the thing must be pieced, and sewn, and draped, to duplicate this impression. You cut, pin, and shape, you extract from this drawing a pattern in toile which will impart three dimensions to a sketch on paper! So Elise Frejon was a cutter, a most valuable employee, fifty years with the firm!"

The women listened, nodding to one another; even a vicarious tour through a fashion house was intriguing. The men were more impatient: "And then?"

"No 'and then'—she was a cutter till the day she died, and my pin lady went to the funeral." Robert was not about to satisfy curiosity except in his own time. "She asked me how I knew Elise Frejon, and I said she was a cousin of my mother's —had *she* any family left? That brought a spate. 'Oh yes, she had a son! Can you imagine! She married very late, he was a functionary of the PTT I believe, and fancy, she had a child— at fifty!' " His voice rose, imitating a staccato falsetto. "You can imagine how we were astonished, but not so astonished as she, poor lady! Still, there it was. She left work for only a month, came back directly after. She brought the baby to work once, in a basket, when the nurse was ill, and there wasn't much work done that day, I can tell you! *Voyons*, M. Richard said we would have to develop a line of baby clothes, Petichic he wanted to call it, and he was as bad as the rest of us, chucking it under the chin!' Well, by now my guide, a dapper young man with a mustache, was standing on one foot and the other, highly impatient, and I still had no firm information. What was her husband's name? I said bluntly, where did she live? She couldn't remember!" His shoulders collapsed in despair; they all groaned in anticipation of yet one more episode.

"But I did not give up." His bald spot rose, twinkling. "If she went to the funeral, had she gone to the house afterward? Oh yes, she had! Everyone had gone, the cutters, the errand boys, the models, even M. Richard—the House was closed for a day of mourning! And many of them had gone to the apartment afterward with the widower and the son. Jacques the son's name was, but he was no longer living with them, a journalist in Marseille. It was there Elise Frejon had been born, did I know that? So no doubt there were relatives there . . . 'Where *was* the apartment?' I said as forcefully as I could manage, and she, 'Oh, of course! It was either the rue Damiette or the rue du Nil, a third- or fourth-floor apartment, near the middle! Surely it was, because I remember when they praised her she used to say, Well, I come from the Cour des Miracles!' "

"Ah!" Marie-Gisèle nodded, gratified, and François; but Marc and Laura looked puzzled. "In the Middle Ages, that was where the beggars and thieves lived . . . it's in *The Hunchback of Notre Dame,* you know. And they called it that because in their off-hours the beggars took off their wooden legs, and the blind could see, and the cripples walked! It's not far from us, Marc, off the rue Réaumur, in the fashion district; remodeled, but some of the old buildings are still there."

Light dawned. "And," said Marc, "you went there and talked to concierges."

"Yes. It was a vain hope, I thought: well, she died at least twelve years ago, and where to begin . . . Do you have *any* idea how many *immeubles* there are in those two short streets, even if you leave off the corner buildings? Nevertheless, for the father of a grandson of unparalleled cleverness . . . do you know that he goes straight for my nose every time, knowing I can be made to honk with it?"

"Yes, yes," said François, not quite rolling his eyes at Laura, "and once more I am extremely grateful! So you talked to endless concierges . . ."

"And climbed stairs, when they were new, to talk to old tenants, asking if they had known an elderly lady named Elise married to a postal functionary, who had worked at the House of . . ."

Marie-Gisèle and Laura exclaimed at once. "But . . ." and Robert grinned his cat's grin. "Oh yes—but that did not occur to me until I had done the rue du Nil and was starting the rue Damiette!" Marc and François looked blank, and Marie-Gisèle said vigorously, "But of course, it's a neighborhood— what they would remember best was that she had a baby when she was fifty!"

"And so they did; and almost immediately after, I had the name Leclerc and a good deal more information I could have done without. This morning I checked the old directories to make sure it was really Leclerc and not Leclaire or Leclère, checked the marriage records—*et voilà!*" And he sat back as if his task were finished.

"Ah non," said Laura, "but the will—you have not explained the will!" "Nor," added François sardonically, "why you so exasperatingly called her *'ladite Edith'* and rang off without telling us why!"

"Ah well, that is another story, and I feel the need to stretch my legs. Trains, you know. Why do we not depart for a less impressive bistro and take a cognac?"

They came out into the night, starless and balmy, and Marie-Gisèle observed sadly, "That is perhaps a tragic story, you know? That miraculous child—and now, if he indeed killed his aunt . . . All her life his mother worked hard, and for what? Do we ever know what our children will bring us? The Protestant ethic—wasn't her mother Protestant? For so much virtue, so little reward!"

"Mm," said Robert. "Well, I am not sure she was as virtuous as all that, you know. The concierge said too that the boy was a gift from heaven, but she added, 'particularly as mademoiselle her daughter died so soon after.' My pin lady knew nothing about that one, and there was no record of a previous marriage, so . . . Ah, now this place is just my style: far better cognac at half the price! This is cognac country you know, the town is not thirty miles from here."

"Eh bien, parle!" François was not about to allow more delay. "Edith and how you knew her—the full story, please!"

"Tiens—'ladite Edith'—your grandmother's name for her, and spoken, I may say, with a bite to it. For your grandfather, François, that Poitiers notary from whom you inherit your taste for the law, had her for a client, and if you believe my grandmother, something more!"

They all exclaimed. It was true that the statement was somewhat inaccurate, since François, Solange's sister's son, was no relation to Robert or Robert's father. But Robert had long been capable of forgetting this completely, and it did not seem the moment to remind him that even his beloved grandson was not his at all. "Then," said Marc, formulating his phrase with an eye to a curious Jouvet, "the grandfather dead, when it came to her will she thought of the grandson."

"I believe that is not an unreasonable presumption, especially as François and his ancestry was dealt with at length in the papers some three years ago . . . I even checked my father's old files in the cellar the night you called, to see whether there was something of interest—but there was nothing, only a carbon of a letter of his to her about some allowance made to her sister. Mind you, I do not necessarily think there was anything in my sainted mother's presumptions about her spouse and Edith! She cast her spell on him, I expect, just long enough to have an inexpensive notary on her string, and it was no inconvenience, having him in Poitiers, since he always went to Paris to see her."

"But how," Marie-Gisèle wanted to know, "did they meet at all?"

"Ah, that I do know." He settled back comfortably for a cozy gossip. "My father, you know, was an artist: in his spare time an aspiring, a lazy, and a very bad painter of impossibly lavish gardens, impossibly blue lakes, and impossibly beautiful women. And, on that account, he had maintained a friendship with a chap from school who was painting, not quite so badly, in Paris. So from time to time he would go up and they would spend a night together talking of nuances and perspective, happy as Bouvard and Pécuchet, or going out to the Quatz' Arts ball or the Deux Magots to hobnob with Bohemia. And it was on one such occasion he met *la belle* Edith, coming across the Boul' Mich' with some director after a performance."

Laura, squinting her eyes, tried to envision it: the two mounting the curb against a background of lights and square cabs and the bustle of the *grand monde*, the St. Jacques Tower gleaming darkly in the background: Edith in the Deux Magots terrace sipping wine, bending lightly toward an awed provincial notary who perceived in her his ultimate destiny . . . Not quite Toulouse-Lautrec, he was too early; but then, there was something inescapably nineteenth century about Edith . . .

"Did you ever meet her?" Marc was curious.

"I saw her, three times. Once, when he took me up for the weekend to Paris—I was perhaps sixteen—and I saw her as the Girl in the Black Velvet Hat: all agog, I was, and Papa and I had a rather embarrassing chat about the birds and the bees afterward. And once, the year before, she came to Poitiers, and my mother asked her to tea."

Marie-Gisèle exclaimed, and he cocked his head at her, "Oh yes, she did . . . and kept her little finger cocked all during the ceremony. I think the intent was to prove a chanteuse from the music hall would not know how to behave in a proper bourgeois environment."

"And did she?"

"Oh yes; she and my father chatted away about the theater, and she complimented my mother upon her Limoges. *I* wanted to ask for her autograph, but didn't quite dare."

"Why not? What was she like, then?" Laura was intent.

Robert whistled between his teeth, thoughtful. "In a way, daunting . . . not beautiful in the conventional sense, the eyes too fierce, the jaw too full; but immense vitality, of course that is always appealing; ego; above all, I suppose, what left one uneasy was a tremendous sense of *will* . . ."

Laura absorbed this, and François asked, curious about the family past, "When was the third time you saw her, then? Did this . . . friendship go on a long time?"

"As a friendship, I believe it did; for the third time I saw her was after the war, about 1957 it would have been. Of course her great success, the one that at the last possible moment almost made her a star, was killed when the war began, and then the fall of Paris . . . She did, I believe, do some good work with the Resistance, though I never ran across her myself; but afterward it was much too late for her to start on the stage again. When she visited Papa, she was shabby-respectable, and she appeared to have aged tremendously. She was extremely upset about something—Mama was dead then—and they were closeted together quite a long time. That was the last time they met, I think."

"And do you know what they talked about?" Marc.

"No. But after she left he shook his head sadly and quoted *Phèdre* at me."

Not surprising, thought Laura: two arrogant women, Phèdre and Edith Lemay, and was there not something Cretan in Edith's profile? And why not? How far from Crete to Marseille? But . . . Racine and Mme. de Maintenon, Racine and Edith Lemay—it was curious how he kept turning up: François had told her what Soeur Richarde planned to do with her legacy!

They walked Robert back to the hotel where they had reserved a room for him, and François said, "Why don't you stay one more day, Papa Rob? Enjoy the beach after your extremely arduous labors!" and the irony was affectionate.

Robert looked up, to where cloud furrows rolled inexorably in, the ominous waves of heaven echoing the sea. "It's not likely to be a good beach day tomorrow—no—I think I will go back to that other miraculous child his parents are so scandalously neglecting. Unless you have some other impossible task for me, to find this nephew, for instance?"

"No, not that," said Marc grimly, "for he was here—staying with us at the villa, and he is due for a session with the examining magistrate tomorrow."

Robert stood stock still, paling under the streetlights. "But why didn't you tell me?—My God, and I found him for you!"

CHAPTER 14

Robert flatly refused to come to the villa for breakfast; it was, he said, bad enough to have tracked the man down without having to face him over mirabelle jam and, moreover, he had an inherent dislike for miraculous children grown into adults . . . Some of Robert's war had not been pleasant, notably a year and a half spent in prison, and when François, at their little café, tried over croissants to cheer him, it was not effective. "You do not really hold any brief for murderers, Papa Rob; and if he is not one you have done him no harm."

"If he is or is not, I will personally have sent him to the examining magistrate and perhaps put him behind bars. I thought I was locating a missing heir for you—today, *c'est toute autre chose!*"

"But," said Laura gently, "to batter an old woman . . ."

"Edith," said Robert firmly, "whoever killed her, undoubtedly asked for it." But he refused to elaborate upon that either.

So they took him to the train and returned, somewhat unhappily, to the villa: none of them, in fact, was overjoyed at the thought of confronting Jacques Leclerc. And the first person they saw, entering, was Jacquot, bouncing his ball in the corridor with immense vigor: "Madame! We did not leave after all! Isn't that splendid! Mama says we cannot afford it, but Papa says we must!—Oh, and monsieur, he was looking for you!"

It was François he addressed; and almost at once Jacques Leclerc appeared at the top of the stairway, distraught and imploring. "M. LeBreton. I must see you—at once if it is possible."

François turned to his companions—if it had to be, the sooner the better. "I don't know how long this will take me—why don't you go and amuse yourselves?"

"You go," said Laura to Marc, when they had disappeared into the bedroom. "I'd rather just . . ."

What she would rather just proved to be walk on the beach and think about this, but on her way out the landlady waylaid her. It was a great inconvenience, the Leclercs' staying over; the room was taken for two days hence; and it was not at all *nice*—did Madame know what the police thought? So the news was all over already! Laura said she did not know what the police thought and as long as M. Leclerc paid his rent she presumed he was entitled to stay there . . .

What a pity! She did not want it to be Jacques Leclerc, and on the empty beach with the air freshening as if clear weather were just over the horizon, she admitted her reasons were sentimental. She did not want Jacquot's father to be a murderer . . . But then, with that father and that mother, Jacquot might not grow up very well in the normal course of things, and a murderer father might just be a deterrent . . . How did one know how children would turn out? Life's consequences were incalculable.

And one must look at the facts. That he was at Pontaillac when his aunt died was at the least an unusual coincidence, and each time she had seen them, the Leclercs had been greatly upset about something. The first time, on Oléron, what had Yvonne said? "Well, if I am crazy, so are you to fear . . ." What? What feminine thing? If she had meant "her," *La Folle,* it would indicate they had not yet known she was dead: but what if it had meant, "her death?" Or "la police?" "Crazy," crazy again his wife had called him at the café—yes, and that must surely have referred to the *Le Monde* article about Edith Lemay. Crazy indeed so to call attention to himself—but, if they needed the money?

Her footsteps had taken her to the far end of the beach, where a treed promontory thrust out to sea and, exasperated

with her own melancholy thoughts, she set out to climb it
. . . But she had not taken half a dozen steps on the crest
before she came on a woman, sitting facing the sea and,
unquestionably, weeping. Her approach had not been heard,
and she turned to withdraw when the other looked up, startled, and said what should have been Laura's line, "Pardon,
madame!"

The accent was unmistakable, and Laura replied in English. "Not at all. I'm sorry . . ."

"Oh, you're American!" It was a cry of relief; she stood, and
Laura delayed her retreat. She was not an unattractive little
woman, ten years older than Laura perhaps, gray-blond hair
carefully permed, the plump chin vulnerable. "Yes, I am; but
I live in France . . . Does that . . ." and she took a step
closer, "help any?"

"Oh, I don't know. Dear Lord, I don't know what to do
about anything!" And she sat down again, in despair. "I'm
such a fool—I guess . . ."

Laura, touched, squatted on heels beside her. "Is it something about travel? Could I translate or be useful to you with
something?" After all, one's compatriots . . .

"I thought for a minute, but I guess . . ." she looked at
Laura mistrustfully. "Are you . . . are you a very *moral* person?"

"Good Lord, no! I've had three husbands and I swear all
the time!" She laughed, and sat down more comfortably.
"Tell me, and if I can help I will."

"Well . . ." the tone was less mistrustful, more confiding,
"I'm a widow, you see, since last year. My sister, my brother-
in-law and I, we're traveling together. It's been interesting,
really, all those museums—and—is it really normal for
Frenchmen just to stand out by the side of the road and . . .
you know?" Laura nodded, comprehending. "Well, that's just
the thing, isn't it, in a foreign country you don't know what's
normal and what isn't!"

"True."

"And it's such a nuisance, being a widow!" She was more

comfortable now. "They have to take me everywhere with them, never have time to themselves, and my brother-in-law . . . Well, I just got tired of people being good to me. So I said I'd go out on my own, and I met this young man in a café, and he was just so . . . Oh, I can't tell you! I am an absolute fool, I just know it, I can't think what came over me!"

"You've been a widow a long time, that's what came over you," said Laura, unexcited, and she seized on it. "Yes—and I'm not old yet . . . or ugly . . . am I?"

"Not a bit. So if things went a bit further than you intended them to—well, you had one night to remember . . . and you haven't lost anything, have you?"

"That's just what I thought. Only"—and it was a wail—"this morning my ruby ring was missing!"

That was another kettle of fish. "You're sure? You just didn't misplace it?"

"Oh, I don't know, how can I? But I have two, the ruby and the opal, and I like the opal better, so—the ruby was on my dresser last night, I'm almost sure. But I was asleep when he —and it could have been the maid, couldn't it? And if I go to the police they'll laugh and my brother-in-law will know and it's all just too awful! I'll never go abroad again!"

Laura had nothing to say. It was just as awful as her new friend suspected: of course she should go to Jouvet, but there would be questions asked at the hotel, and the staff would tap its head and say, "crazy American," and it would be a snicker all over Royan . . . "And," said the little blonde percipiently, "they'll know all over Bloomfield Hills too, my sister can't keep her mouth shut for anything. So I guess"— and a basic shrewdness hardened her face through the dried tears—"I'll just say for a night of love it came higher than I thought it would and remember that next time!"

"All the same"—Laura was not quite happy—"You ought to say. I have a friend in the police here . . . if I just mentioned it . . ."

"No!" Her mind made up, her tone was harder. "We're leaving tomorrow, and I'm not staying around for anything

. . . I appreciate what you said, but I could see you knew as well as I do . . ." She stood. "Goodbye, and if you ever repeat what I said—I know you won't, but if you ever do—I'll just say you made it all up, that's all!" And she made off through the trees as fast as her narrow heels would carry her.

Laura turned back, troubled, reflecting: so nasty a tale one did not quite know what to do with it. Surely Jouvet should be told—but if the woman refused to confirm it? And she did not even have her name, the hotel where she was staying, much less a description of the young man, the name of the café where she met him. Too late now; she was gone . . . Well, she would tell Marc, anyway, and he would say, "What do you expect me to do with that?" and he would be in the right of it . . . Crossing back to the villa, she saw Jean Calvet and his wife returning from tennis, undaunted by clouds, and was struck again by the impression of oneness that emanated from the double-proud profile—even their rackets swung in unison: surely Germaine Moreuil was mistaken.

Jacques Leclerc was, clearly, a man in the last extremities of anxiety, and François thought briefly how apt, after all, had been Robert's description: "a miraculous child grown to adult." No doubt he had been thoroughly spoiled, had never learned how to shoulder his own problems: and now, equally beyond doubt, they were going to descend on François. "Well, M. Leclerc, and to what do I owe the honor of this visit?"

"You must act for me! It is imperative! Without you I am lost, I know it!" The journalist's appeal verged on hysteria, yet in the tone there was a habitual ring of self-serving, as from one who knew that if you despaired instantly you need make no effort, there would always be someone to save you. It was not an approach calculated to appeal to François.

"Well, M. Leclerc, I will do what I can for you, but at this stage . . ."

"If not at this stage, then at the trial—and that will be too late for me!" And he sat down, without invitation, his hands hanging between his knees in dejection.

"Surely not! That you are—I presume you are—Edith Lemay's heir may well cause suspicion, but that alone could hardly . . ."

"Ah, but there is"—his arm flung out to embrace the universe—"all the evidence in the world against me. When all is known I am finished, I know it! And yet, M. LeBreton, I swear I am innocent!"

"Gently. Let us, if you will, examine the situation. You came here with what purpose: by accident?"

"No, no. There is no secret about our coming. You see," and here he became confiding, child at his mother's knee confessing transgressions, "we needed money. Six months ago I lost my post—a disagreement of principle with my editor—but he need not have been, need he, quite so drastic about it? Well, I will find something else soon, I said to myself, a good journalist never lacks work, but somehow . . . The economy is not in a good state, you know, and the expenses . . . Well, if one wants a job one must go where other journalists are and buy a drink for the fellows—Yvonne just does not understand that! And Jacquot—you have no idea how expensive a child is!"

No, but I shall soon, thought François to himself, and aloud, "So you were short of money?"

"Yes." He leaned forward eagerly. "And Yvonne said—well, we knew I was her heir, didn't we? She said, 'Maybe your aunt will help you, even find you a job, she must have contacts. An old lady like that, what can her needs be? We will take the rest of our savings and go to Royan with Jacquot for a few days, let the old lady become acquainted with him, they always enjoy children! And then when the moment is ripe, you can ask for a loan.'"

"And you?"

"I thought she was mad," he said frankly. "What, the rest of our savings on a chance like that? But she is clever, Yvonne, a good manager, and sometimes . . . besides, she is stubborn!

For Jacquot, I believe, she would roast her own grandmother." Man-to-man. "What could I say? We came."

"And then?"

"Well, we arrived, and . . . and . . ."

"And what?"

"We walked on the beach and spent an enjoyable day out of doors . . ."

A recalcitrant witness, but not in the box, thank God! François had no patience. "Well then, did you see your aunt or not? You were here two days before she was killed, I think!"

He looked about the room. "Yvonne is sometimes very unreasonable. She wanted me to go the first day, but I had to think how I would present myself, didn't I? After all, you can hardly ask for a loan at once, and I had to give a reason why . . . If she thought I had come only for money, she might even get angry and disinherit me! It required tact! So then the second night she said I must go now, right after dinner, and invite *her* to dinner at the villa the next day. So I went—and I know the police will discover it, I asked a passerby where her house was, and then they will be sure I killed her, and it will be the guillotine!" He wrung his hands, fingers writhing unpleasantly. "If only I had not listened to her!"

"You went, and what happened?"

"She was not at home! I swear to you, the door never opened!"

"What time was this?"

"About nine, I think—my watch is unfortunately in repair . . ."

Pawned, said François to himself, and nine was much too early; if the passerby could be found . . . but that did not prevent his returning, and as yet the police had no idea he was there at all! "And the rest of the night?"

"I was with Yvonne, of course!"

A sigh. Motive, no alibi, for everyone knew wives lied for their husbands and even more for inheritance: a messy case, unrewarding.

"Well, now, M. Leclerc, I can only advise you to be frank

with the police and with the magistrate, up to a point. You came for a holiday, you planned to visit your aunt, it was not urgent, you called at the house, and she was not at home. I think we may risk that. Someone will, as you say, have seen you, better it should be learned from you. What does require explanation, what does look odd, is your not coming forward when you learned she was dead. How do you explain that?"

"Oh, I have already told the commissaire." He seemed naively proud of this. "I said to Yvonne we must leave at once, go home and pretend we had never been here. But *she* said no, they would find out, we *must* stay, and perhaps discover who had really killed her. And if I went to the police, they would look no further, so I must not do that. Besides, we had paid for a week, hadn't we? So she scouted about, and I'm afraid," he looked embarrassed, "suspected your wife, when she learned of the necklace. But she thought others, too . . ."

François shook his head, unbelieving. "And what did Commissaire Jouvet say when you told him this?"

"He said—well, I did not tell him the first part, but I explained about wanting to find the real murderer, and he was much struck by it!"

Yes, I can believe he was! François's lips expelled air . . . If there was ever an incompetent, dishonest, unreliable . . . But clients did not, as a rule, enter his study in shining armor, and if Jacques Leclerc had indeed killed his aunt, the impulse could only have come from the Lady Macbeth behind him. "M. Leclerc—you understand that as your aunt's lawyer, circumstances may arise which will make it impossible for me to act for you. But in the meantime, I will do what I can."

"Thank you, monsieur; I do most gratefully thank you!" He pumped François's hand. "With your skill, your reputation, I feel confident that—Oh! Yvonne told me to be sure to ask you: now that we must stay on, we are a little short of cash, as you may imagine—would it be possible—in the estate there is, perhaps, this emerald necklace?"

"That is not clear." François was firm. "And, at the mo-

ment, it is in the police safe." Let him think they had impounded it as evidence, he was not about to hand over emerald necklaces! "Besides the house, there was very little, but I
will speak to the landlady . . ."

And he closed the door after a Jacques Leclerc become
suddenly debonair, cheerful.

CHAPTER 15

"Well, did he do it, or not?" inquired Marc over supper.

"Now how, as his lawyer—or halfway his lawyer—do you expect me to answer that? He says not—and if it comes to Leclercs, I would put my money on the lady of the household!" Laura watched him, unconscious of what her face revealed: his mind was so precise an instrument, yet never arid; sensitive, delicate; what she thought, he perceived before she could formulate it, yet never said so unless it were necessary. True, it went away from her sometimes, that mind, wrapped in a brown study; and she, at the core a solitary herself, let him be: was it not all the more delightful when he laughed, as now, light rippling on a clear spring? "How can you tell anything with these—these sliding people? They can make *themselves* believe a lie is the truth! If, exasperated by his wife, he struck out at his aunt, he is perfectly capable of thinking it was his wife he struck, yet not really, for there she stands intact! I don't want him for a client if I can help it."

"*She* was not like that, Edith Lemay," said Laura suddenly. "I think—a very direct person."

"Perhaps he gets it from his father . . . These bureaucrats . . ." Marie-Gisèle felt a passing interest. "But you know, unless he had planned to kill her, he would not go back late in the evening, it might annoy her; and if he *did* plan to kill her why go so early in the first place?"

"And it does not explain"—the moment still haunted Laura—"why she was so distressed, in front of the villa—he was not even there. And if she had recognized Yvonne and

Jacquot, surely she would have rushed up, said, 'Oh my, what a surprise, have you come to visit me?' It is not logical."

"Neither are madwomen." Marc was sardonic.

"Oh, but they are. It is just that their logic is not ours." Marie-Gisèle nodded.

"And the emerald necklace? She left that to me as a senti-mental memory of François's grandfather? Pooh. She meant something by that, but what? What *can* a necklace mean? Jewels?—Oh, that reminds me!" And she told Marc of her curious beach encounter.

He frowned and scolded, as she expected, at the paucity of her information. "Nevertheless I'll tell Jouvet, it's his turf, after all."

"I was taken by surprise," Laura defended herself. "Who expects strange women to burst upon one in coppices and tell you their love lives?"

"I do," said Marc, "or rather, I long for them. Police work consists of long periods in which nobody will tell you any-thing—but you, Laura! . . . Perhaps if I pretended to be an American?"

"No." Marie-Gisèle was amused. "I won't have strange women unbosoming themselves to you—although that chest-nut seller today, in front of the church—what a front eleva-tion! One imagined the pair of them gently smoking there, over the fire, for years and years—it would be quite an exotic experience, don't you think? Oh, but I didn't tell you, Laura, we have seen a *little* Romanesque church, and it was ador-able! So tough and so graceful, and all those little carved people with big heads and no faces—it was like a church dollhouse! Can we not make a Romanesque tour tomorrow?"

François agreed heartily, as much to avoid the Leclercs as from an interest in churches, Laura suspected; but they were not to get off so easily. On the stairs the next morning the landlady detained them: "M. LeBreton, I believe you are M. Leclerc's lawyer."

"No, I have merely given him some advice in a temporary capacity."

But this did not stop her. "Nevertheless, I must tell you that it is not nice to have police in the house, searching, my principals would not like it at all! And I wondered if you might not tell M. Leclerc that I would appreciate it if he and his family sought other lodgings!"

"Madame, I am not a bailiff. If you wish him to leave, you must tell him yourself. All I can do is assure you your bill will be paid."

"Ah!" That made a difference, it seemed, and she retreated to her office to think it over. And then it was the Moreuils who, learning of their proposed expedition at breakfast, greeted it so enthusiastically they were invited to join the party. "But we must go in my car, no, I insist, it is a large Citroën," declared the professor, immediately taking charge of the expedition; and while they spread out maps, planning a route, Laura sought out Jean in the porter's lodge.

It was scarcely more than a closet, with telephone, a *caisse* for keys and messages, and just room enough underneath to leave a suitcase. But there was a tiny desk and, sure enough, a shark's tooth lay amid the pens and papers. "The little Leclerc boy, Jean, says that Mme. Lemay telephoned you the afternoon before she was killed. Is that true?"

Jean looked up, surprised, and came to the half-door. "*Voyons*, was that . . . ? But yes, of course you are right! I had forgotten. Do the police want to . . ."

"No, no. I suppose it's of no importance at all; but I wondered—she wanted to know who was staying here?"

"Yes, madame." He squinched his eyes, concentrating. " 'Jean, this is Mme. Lemay. Can you tell me who is staying at the villa at this moment?' Well, it is confidential more or less, but a lady like that, one did not like to argue; and besides, I knew she meant no harm, did she? So I read her the names."

"And did she say anything?"

"Well yes—a comment about each one, as one does with a list, while the other person is looking . . . For the Antonionis it was 'Italian, I suppose,' and the Bernsteins—they left the next day, 'Ah, Boches.' When I came to you she said

'*Tiens!*' and for the Leclercs—that was her nephew, was it not, madame—she did not seem to take particular notice. But it is of course a common name, isn't it?"

"And who else did you mention?"

"The Moreuils, and that surprised her: '*Extraordinaire!*' I think she said. But throughout she seemed a little surprised and distracted, as if thinking of some other urgent matter. I left the Calvets till the last, not being sure whether I would mention them—he, you know, prefers anonymity—but she said nothing, just repeated the name."

Laura turned away satisfied that Jacquot's report had been accurate—but it was curious and confirmed surely that Edith Lemay's shock on the sidewalk had been *recognition.* But which, and why? Remembering, she turned back once more. "And M. Machicoulet and his friend—did you mention them?"

"No, madame, because they had not yet registered." Could that, perhaps, be why she had not reacted especially strongly to one name? And yet—it was after that phone call, Laura was certain, that Edith Lemay had gone to her bureau, inscribed her will to François's attention, and added the codicil that left the emerald pendant to Laura.

And so they went touring. The circuit of Romanesque churches which Michelin recommends begins at Saintes and covers a circle of fifty miles, but it took the holiday party all day. Corme-Royal, Sablonceaux, Thaims, Retaud, Rioux, and then it seemed foolish not to extend their sightseeing a little farther and take in Fontdouce, Ecoyeux, and the Château de Cazannes. The day was gentle, the sun glowing delicately through a faint mist drifted in from the sea; caressing, it bathed the dovecote towers, the blind arches, the deep doorways of churches where village life had focused for seven centuries, and laid its benison upon the fields about the sharp tower of Sablonceaux, the ruins of Fontdouce . . . The professor spoke learnedly of barrel vaults, tribunes, and reinforcing double arches, but it was the sculpture that fascinated

Marie-Gisèle: the Retaud grotesques, the three-headed god at Fontdouce, the wild men at Cazannes. "Your Celtic blood stirs," said Moreuil, only half-joking, "your three-headed god was Celtic before he entered an abbey, and the wild men . . . Do you remember the Bacchic stone at Thaims, and the memorial to the goddess Epona? Thaims was Roman before it was Romanesque, and before that undoubtedly a local Celtic cult center. The beliefs of two thousand years or more cluster in these sanctuaries."

"And were they," Laura wanted to know, "all on the pilgrim route to Compostela?"

"Some, yes. One major road ran down from Tours to Aulnay—which has also a very beautiful church, I believe. The two others from northern parts met at St. Jean d' Angély and Saintes. Half a million a year, those pilgrims in cloak and scallop shell. Not all on this route, of course, but surely a hundred thousand. It took a great many churches and abbeys to shelter them, and they spread out in the countryside. There was even a Pilgrim Guide, the ancestor of our Michelin, which told them the routes, the road markers, the climate, the customs of the inhabitants and, no doubt, which abbey served the best cuisine!" And he laughed cheerfully.

Even Marc was impressed. "And why, for heaven's sake? What did they expect to find at Compostela?"

"Who knows? The bull of the story is certainly older than the Christian saint in it. Compostela may have been holy as long as there were men to visit it. And if someone tells you at the end of some *route nationale* there is some magic elixir, will you not go see?"

Marc considered. "No. I am a practical man, and I do not believe in magic of any kind. Even about salvation I am not quite certain."

Germaine joined in the game. "But then you must remember the joys of travel, seeing new places, meeting new people . . . Consider our annual August descent of the whole north of Europe upon the Riviera! Like lemmings! And there is not even a hope of salvation at the end of it!"

They all agreed, laughing, and Laura said downright, "I cannot understand when people sneer at a pilgrimage when it is scientific fact that even a mile walk a day will lengthen your life and raise your spirits into the bargain! It is the age we live in, narrow-minded and incredibly stupid!"

It was evening when they returned to Saintes, after lingering for a walk in the gardens of the Château de Douhet; and the sextet dined together in a restaurant on the north side of the city. Now that Pontaillac loomed closer, the conversation drifted inevitably to their cause célèbre, and both the professor and Germaine seemed intently interested, if at cross-purposes. "Is it true," Germaine wanted to know, "that Leclerc was really her nephew, and that is why the police are questioning him?" Marc nodded. "Good!" Her tone was of heartfelt satisfaction. "Then they have caught the murderer, and we can forget all about it!"

"Germaine"—the professor looked weary, as if all that walking had been too much for him—"they are questioning him only—a man is innocent until proven guilty—So, for that matter, is a woman. And even if it were he, I am certain she would not have wanted him punished."

"And why not?" she turned on him. "That it was in the family makes it worse, not better, surely?"

"Her only blood descendant, add sorrow to sorrow? And indeed, he did not seem to me the sort of fellow to murder, much less to take jewels from a dying woman's body!"

"No," agreed Marie-Gisèle. "Why would he take them, if he was going to inherit them anyway? Oh, I suppose . . . to make it look like a robbery. But surely to kill your own aunt, you would have to dislike her? Too? What kind of person she was, that's what I wonder, and the newspapers tell you nothing. The Girl in the Black Velvet Hat—well, what was it?"

The professor opened his mouth to reply, but his wife forestalled him. "Oh, my dear, that I can tell you—it was the first French *strip-tease!*"

They all exclaimed in surprise and waited. "Well, then— the Americans had had *le strip-tease*, I think, for a long time, but it was not in the French tradition. Knees, yes; bosoms, yes; *le tout nu*, never. In the thirties, however, what was American was all the rage in the music halls, and she decided, I suppose, to take advantage of it." "Not she, Santorini," the professor said crossly. "Just as you like, my dear—you saw it and I didn't. But I am *told*"—and she gave Michel a glance that held more than anger at his interruption—"that it was on the whole tasteful: a sort of skit, and a song that went with it, '*sans formalités*' or something . . ."

" '*Tu me connais,* Madame Sans-Gêne.' " The professor.

"That's right, I remember . . . She came onstage fully costumed, absolutely Edwardian, long skirt, buttoned bodice, cloak, gloves, I don't know what: the perfect lady taking time out from shopping to visit her lover. And it was very well done, it appears; one could almost see him. She shook hands—did he object to her gloves? She would remove them. Did he like her dress? No? Then away with it! And her petticoat? *Je l'enlève—tu me connais*—Madame Sans-Gêne.' And in the end there she was, nothing but herself and this enormous magnificent black velvet hat, the only thing he had not objected to. Oh, it was quite the rage, I assure you!"

"She was," said the professor in measured tones, "not quite, all the same, nude: and it was, in her career, the most unfortunate moment. How anyone, after that, could admire her real talent! But Santorini . . ."

"Just so, my dear; I know you have *read* a great deal about the music hall. But lives like that . . . do they not, often . . . end badly?" And she seemed quite convinced of the correctness of her judgment.

Back at the villa François, suffering from a surfeit of fresh air, went directly to bed; but Laura went into the salon to find something to read. Gilbert Machicoulet was just taking his leave of Mme. Calvet, kissing her hand with *empressement,* so Laura stepped back; but Mme. Calvet greeted her with a warmth that was unexpected. "Good night, Gilbert."

It was a dismissal. "Mme. LeBreton, stay a minute, I have things I wanted to ask you."

Laura sat down in the easy chair on the other side of the window table and waited. "Now can you tell me, *entre nous,* what is the truth of the talk about this little journalist? I realize perhaps it is not within your discretion, but . . . I am concerned for my husband, you see. He is always, unfortunately, of interest to the public, and if this man were to be arrested—well, you can see the headlines, can't you? 'Calvet and Murderer Under Same Roof.' 'Calvet Says He Scarcely Knew Assassin'—most disagreeable!" She was lucid and firm, and her tone reminded Laura of Germaine Moreuil—but no, Germaine in youth would not have been like this woman. Shy, self-conscious about her size, Germaine would have gained confidence only with maturity; in age, Mme. Calvet would either learn serenity or she would be impossible. "I don't know what I can tell you," said Laura thoughtfully, "except that it is no secret M. Leclerc was Mme. Lemay's nephew."

"Her nephew!" The information shocked her, and Laura had the impression of plans already marshaled coming under rapid review. "Then—we must move, I suppose. Oh, what a nuisance! And I chose this place because it seemed so quiet, anonymous—now, if there is scandal, it will certainly be my fault." She sighed, eyes haunted, and Laura felt sorry for her. She was not, close up, as young as she had first appeared: late twenties to her husband's fifties perhaps—and not as remote. It was true that the Calvets had held themselves apart, but why not? A life like theirs must be full of official and sociopolitical engagements, and two weeks almost alone together might well seem paradise. "Still—it may not be as serious as you think. There is nothing so far but the relationship to involve him—no real evidence—he says he went to see her that night and returned shortly after nine, which was before the murder—and if it can be proved that he did not go out later . . ."

Mme. Calvet looked startled, and her next remark startled

Laura. "But—I saw him return! Yes, I am sure I did! My husband, you know, had gone out to meet some people, a political affair, and I was standing at the window tapping my fingers wondering what to do, when . . . yes, it was then he came up the walk. He is going bald on the top of his head, have you noticed? It was full light still then, my husband had left at eight—about an hour before—yes, it would have been about nine-twenty."

This was confirmation indeed, but it did not clear Jacques Leclerc yet. "And—were you in all evening? He would scarcely have gone out again through the kitchen—did you hear him leave afterward?"

"Oh, my dear, how could I possibly . . . ! And yet . . ." She frowned, eyes half-closed, remembering. "A great many people came *back* between ten and eleven: our rooms are in front, overlooking the sea, but the stairs are a bit noisy. The professor and his wife, the Antonionis, Gilbert and his friend —I was reading, and I remember thinking"—she smiled ruefully—"that everyone *else* was out enjoying the evening! But I could almost swear no one went *down* the stairs!"

"Could you swear it, if it came to a trial?"

Her nose wrinkled in a moue of distaste. "A trial! Jean would certainly not like . . . and neither would I! But you can tell your husband what I have said, if you like, and if it ever comes to that we will talk, he and I!"

CHAPTER 16

Next morning at breakfast there was no Marie-Gisèle, and Marc said, in the plaintive tone of a child whose mother has abandoned him, "She tells me that not for ten years has she been able to spend a morning in bed, and this is the morning. So I am on my own—if you two will have me."

"Nonsense," said François briskly, "a marvelous chance to go fishing again—and this time *I* may get one too. Out on the sea alone—without criminals, without clients . . ."

"But Laura—what will she do?"

"Laura knows perfectly well how to amuse herself." But afterward, in the room, he asked, "You really don't mind, do you? You can go shopping, prowl about—have lunch with Marie-Gisèle when she gets tired of bed?"

"Oh yes—I can find plenty to do, don't worry!"

"Yes—you will wander about and talk to anyone you find—murderers, jewel thieves! Don't think I don't know you are still very curious about these people." And he touched her cheek gently.

She entwined her fingers with his: "Yes, it is a curious cat you have married! But I will come to no harm in broad daylight!"

She took the car, nevertheless, to the Préfecture—one ought not to walk the streets carrying in one's purse an emerald necklace. For she had known at once what she would do with the morning: take the necklace to someone who might be expert in the meaning of jewels.

And at the Préfecture they made no difficulties when she said she was taking it to a jeweler for appraisal. "Only drive with care, madame," said Sarrazin, "we do not want our

emeralds in an accident, do we? And if I may suggest, ———'s
in Royan is the best place locally."

Royan was not, of course, the rue de la Paix, but on holiday
people are expansive, they shop, sometimes they even buy
jewels. Often enough, at any rate, to support one jeweler of
elegance, and when she entered the atmosphere was gratify-
ingly discreet and luxurious. An appraisal? She took out the
necklace, inappropriately wrapped in Kleenex—ah, for that
she should have M. Pierre.

M. Pierre wore a black suit, and the tips of his mustache
gleamed sharp as diamonds. *"Oui*, madame, certainly? It is
yours, then? You know its provenance?"

Laura explained why not—that it was part of an estate her
husband was administering—". . . and it would be useful to
know soon what its value is—whether indeed it is an emerald
or perhaps paste! You would be paid, of course, for the appraisal, and we would certainly pay more if you are able to
establish its antecedents. The owner was not rich, and before
it goes to the heirs it would be well to be sure that . . ."
Mendacious, but Edith Lemay had not willed her this elegant
trinket just so that she might ignore its history.

"Of course, madame." He affixed his loupe trimly. "I can
tell you now that it is a very fine emerald, close to four carats
—a sizable gift to the heirs! Then, of course, the diamonds in
the setting . . . As for the source, it may just be possible to
discover that. This is not, you understand, a purchase *d'occasion:* it was made, in all probability, for a particular person,
about fifty years ago: and there were at that time only three
men in France likely to have created it."

"Why do you say that?"

"It is clear. The setting for the pendant, in its twining,
contains initials: on the left, here, you see an *E* concealed
amid the leaves and ribbon, and something on the other side
also. It is the lover's knot theme in a new variant—one finds it
often in medieval work such as Anne de Bretange's initials in
the Unicorn Tapestries. And that suggests also it may have
been a wedding gift . . ."

"What is it, the other initial?"

"I cannot be sure." They peered at it, heads meeting. "A *C,* perhaps? a *G?* or even an *L.* It is a long time since it was made, of course, but if Madame wishes me to make inquiries?"

Madame did. "Then, with your permission, I shall put it in the safe pending an exact appraisal and give you a receipt for it. Is it insured?"

"I have no idea."

"Then—I think I shall insure it for the week or two I will have it—the charge for that, of course, will go on the appraisal."

A week or two! That would not do at all. She wheedled. "If it is at all possible—can we have it by Thursday? There is a meeting with the heir then, and . . ."

His eyebrows went up, and the cost of the appraisal with it. Well, no matter: Edith Lemay would have wanted her to. "I will if I can, madame . . . telephone me."

But I must, she said to herself, departing, not forget to tell François where the necklace is now; and, making a mental note, head down, she ran straight into the professor.

"M. Moreuil! I am sorry!"

"No, not at all—at my age, it is pleasant to have any sort of contact with a pretty woman. But what are you doing in Royan?"

"Some matters concerned with Mme. Lemay's estate . . ."

He looked at the facade behind her. "Then the thief did not get all her jewels! . . . Well, since we have met, will you take a coffee?"

She would and, when they had been served, looked at him directly. "M. Moreuil, will you tell me what you know about Edith Lemay?"

He looked at her, disconcerted. "Well, if I can . . . but you know . . . what I said yesterday . . ."

"Oh no. You know more than that, I think. I think you knew her."

He opened his mouth, closed it, and sighed. "Yes, of course," he said wearily. "Germaine has insisted I say nothing at all, that what I know makes no difference; but I expect I have given myself away more than once, eh?" He looked out over the harbor where, beyond bathers and white sails, the navy blue line of the horizon translated man's works into a timeless immensity. "Perspective . . . yes, perhaps, at last I can set it in its true perspective, God knows at my age . . . Well then, you must know that many years ago, when I was a boy of sixteen, I was not very attractive. I had, even then, a passion for facts, collections of facts, unrelated to any practical purpose, and I was, I imagine, as unrelated to life as they were.

"My father dismissed me, his only child, as an unfortunate oddity; my mother tolerated but could not love me, I had no friends, only my cousin Charlie . . .

"How can I describe him? Everything I was not, gay, clever with people, talented . . . He was six years older than I, and for reasons I still do not comprehend, he took an interest in me. When I was small I followed him everywhere, and I suppose he was flattered. The age difference was just right: he was neither rival nor parent: and it amused him, from time to time, to take me in hand, to further my true education as a brother would. Does that make sense to you?" He looked at her directly, and she nodded: oh yes; a critical relationship, one of the most critical, perhaps, in Michel Moreuil's life. "And so?"

"And so that fall he took me to see Edith Lemay peform. It must have been nearly the beginning of their relationship; she had not yet used one of his songs, but they were discussing it. This would have been . . . 1924, perhaps. It was a stirring time in the music hall world, I can tell you, a watershed . . . I first saw her at one of the smaller halls, which did not last long, and that was the music hall as it used to be: trained seals from Russia, wire walkers from Italy, sword-swallowers from Estonia mixed in with the stand-up comics, the musicians and the girls—even the pianist did a number with his nose! But we had already, then, seen the first of the musical comedies, the first of the big reviews, Mistinguett and American jazz, Trenet and the contemporary ballad. And she, at that moment, was out of place in either. Ah, I remember her in her long skirt and middy blouse, still looking faintly prewar, you know! with the hem-lifting and the flick of the ankle at the naughty bits of the song: and that aquiline nose and that little sensual fullness at the root of her jaw . . . Power, she had power, and not only of the voice; and I saw at once what Charlie saw, she was the wrong *shape* for what she was doing. So we remade her, Charlie and I."

"How?"

"The songs were Charlie's . . . Oh, he would have been wasted as a lawyer, all his classes at the École de Droit . . . but as a songwriter, catchy, provocative, lyric, he could capture the moment in the twist of a note, or a word. You've heard Piaf . . . He could have been the French Cole Porter, and he knew it. What he needed was a voice, a vehicle. And what she needed was a style, a trademark.

"Charlie provided the style, but the trademark was mine, the bottle green velvet dress which made her a chanteuse . . . Ah, even now when I see that shade, that texture in a shop window, I turn, I go back to look at it . . . Once I saw it on the street in an afternoon suit, and I followed that lady all the way to Buttes-Chaumont!"

Heady: heady stuff indeed, for a misanthropic adolescent— creating a nightclub singer! "And was she happy to be remade?"

"Oh yes. She was not stupid, you know, and she was already an old trouper. Even before the war ended she had been a performer in London, with Cochran—he was a famous producer of international talent, launched Delysia in England . . . She came back to Paris with *Chu Chin Chow,* and when it folded she stayed: her family was there, though I think she did not see much of them. Her mother was very strict, and when they moved to Paris during the war she . . . slipped the leash, so to speak. The stage was her life's blood, she could do anything, skits, dance, song; and she possessed that mysterious quality which makes an audience sit up and take notice: she had presence." He dreamt a moment.

"And you and Charlie?"

"Oh, of course. Charlie played the piano, got her engagements; I came when I could and almost every Sunday night, when she was at leisure, I spent with them. They were lovers by then, of course; she was two years older than he but it scarcely mattered. They were partners and she adored him. 'My genius! my poet! we shall become famous together!' she would say, waving the spaghetti spoon—she was a good southern cook, ratatouille, spaghetti, and always enough for three helpings. 'Take another plateful, Michel—all that brainwork—it takes a lot of spaghetti to make a brilliant scholar!' We were her mentors, but also her children; she loved to hug us as we sat, our thinking heads buried for the moment in the splendid pillow of her bosom! Oh, I cannot tell now . . ." he smiled wryly, "whether it was the spaghetti or the bosom, but it was the only place in the world where I never felt hungry!"

The earthly paradise . . . most people had one, often in early childhood, and Laura was never sure if it were blessing or curse . . . Her own, like the professor's, had come later, the years from twelve to sixteen when there was only her father and herself, hunting, hiking and, at home, cooking and discussing his work together . . . All the serious mistakes of her life had sprung from the effort to recapture it, and in particular her two marriages. Harry, with his bonhomie, his enthusiastic hello to life—and his alcoholism; Paul, who had seemed to want a marriage of equals and who had deceived her in that as in all else . . . The professor seemed to have done better; without that warmth at a critical time would he ever have achieved career, marriage, satisfaction?

And as if reading her thoughts he said, "It was then my collections of facts first came into their own: they made Charlie laugh, and she respected them. She seemed to share my feeling that a fact was a tool, you tucked it away in case sometime it might make the difference between life and death: or in her case, success or failure. She herself was a collector: every scrap of information about the stage, past and present, she stored away like a pack rat—thousands of old ballads, for instance. But she knew there was a wider world too, that she had not grasped and never would without formal education. I was a channel to it. And she pushed me out from the fact itself: Why was a sperm whale called a sperm whale? And if we threw coins in a fountain because our Celtic ancestors had, why had *they* done it? She asked questions constantly and I had to go find the answers: without her, my life might never have run into constructive channels."

"And how long did your intimacy last, the three of you?"

"Five years. Oh, things had begun to go wrong before that. I would come, and Charlie would be sleeping, or there would be no food in the house; if he was awake, she would often rail at him. He had not turned up, or a new song was not finished, why? I blamed her; I did not understand, and when she finally told me it was, I think, an act of desperation. Charlie had become an addict—cocaine—even then, you know, it was fashionable among musicians. I didn't believe it, and to the extent I did I believed, naively, that if she loved him as I did he would not do this . . . In the end she left him, and two weeks later they picked Charlie up on the banks of the Seine, dead of an overdose and exposure."

Laura exclaimed, under her breath. "And then?"

"I went to see her, of course, at the hotel where she was lodging. I thought . . . I don't know what I thought, but I knew only we two could share this, whether I accused her, wept with her, proposed to her . . . Yes, I even thought of marriage, young as I was; I had the sense that she needed protection. I had no chance to do any of them; she told me to go away. 'I am through with all that—the first *rich* man I find, I'll take him.' I must have shown what I thought, because she almost spat at me. 'Well, what would you have me do, Michel? I am twenty-eight years old, and my one chance to get to the top has betrayed me. How many more years do you think Charlie has left me? I have to look after myself; no one else is going to!' And she shut the door in my face."

"And was that the end of your relationship? Did you ever see her again?"

"Yes, once . . . There *were* rich men, I think, and the Girl in the Black Velvet Hat was part of that, which is why I detest it . . . I did my best not to know anything. 'Twenty Years of Music Hall,' however . . . I had found Germaine then, my life was in a very good period, I thought, this once, I can afford to. She sang two of Charlie's songs, and I had to leave in the middle. It was not only my own pain, I heard her pain as she sang them, and I forgave her, if there was anything that needed forgiveness. 'Well, perhaps she now has it, the fame she sought,' I said to myself. And from that time until we came here, I never spoke to her."

CHAPTER 17

Laura perched haunch on the edge of Marie-Gisèle's bed: a lady of luxury about to begin the day, she stretched, sat up, hands about knees, and said, "Just think of it! No men till evening: and we can have lunch just where we please! And what will you bet I can guess what *you* have been doing—engaging innocent fellow residents in talk, hoping to find an assassin!"

Laura picked up Marie's novel, which had slid from bedclothes to floor. "Not exactly—and I'm sure anything I can do Marc could do much better! But I cannot help being—curious after that one sight of her."

"After Paul and all that, you don't feel . . . ?" She let it hang in the air, delicately; when your friend has seen one husband killed before her eyes by another, you are careful about saying so bluntly.

"Put off? Horrified? . . . No. I didn't see her die—didn't even see her dead body . . . and of course I never knew her."

"But you think she knew someone who lives at the villa now, and that may have something to do with it. Well, let me see. You know all about us and the Leclercs," she was teasing now, steering away from deep waters, "who have you been quizzing this morning?"

"The professor, actually." And she told Marie-Gisèle the essence of their conversation. "Truly!" said Marie-Gisèle, deeply impressed. "He did know her—was even, from what you say, in love with her? *Tiens!*"

"Yes, and it helped me to understand *her* much better. But

he—he would scarcely have had a reason, after so long: he had forgiven her, probably forgotten."

Marie-Gisèle looked wise. "Ah, I would not go so far as that! Supposing . . . supposing the whole experience left other marks on him! Supposing, for instance, he found he could never make love to another woman—the Moreuils have no children, do they! Something like that could rankle a whole life long, and suddenly seeing her . . ."

It was Laura's turn to be impressed; she would never have thought of that. "I'm not sure that he did, though; on the walk, his back would have been to her. He did say one curious thing, however—how did it go—from then until he came here, he never spoke to her. It was, I thought, an odd wording: it could mean he did speak to her after they came here, or even . . ."

"Or even that he had written to her! Perhaps often, perhaps in a threatening way! And it was to get away from him that she came to Royan . . . He searched the house to get his hands on those letters . . . Oh, he is still a candidate, our professor: and in a way, it is a tribute to both of them. Can you imagine, at eighty-three, being killed in a crime of passion; at seventy-seven, killing for love? . . . But what would he kill her with? It was, wasn't it, something narrow and slightly curved . . ."

"His cane, that he never uses?" Laura remembered what his wife had once said. "But no, there was plastic . . ."

"Et mon plastique! My raincoat!" The voice came from the stairs, descending, and it was Germaine's. "I saw you pack it" —the professor was patient, replying—"I am sure it will turn up somewhere!" It was a curious coincidence, and Marie-Gisèle sobered. "But you realize," she said in a lowered voice, "if what we were guessing was true, it would give her a motive also."

"Bah," said Laura uneasily—she liked Germaine Moreuil— "it is only a game, Marie. After all, there is no real reason to suppose it was any of us who killed her—she might have even just felt faint with the heat!"

"No, no, I prefer it to be so!" She was teasing again, lightly. "The English country house, the closed list of suspects, *tout à fait classique, n'est-ce pas?* And remember, you are nowhere near finished with your interrogations. Gilbert and his friend Mathieu—and the Calvets! It will be difficult to cross-question Jean Calvet I think; I would not try it. And the Italians!" For there they were now, like a herd of large animals clambering the steps to the third floor. "But in such a mob, papa, mamma, the brother and his wife, the two maids, the six children and grandmamma, I think it would be very difficult to do anything privately! But now let us dress and in all elegance find a café to display ourselves!"

Laura changed too: there was a certain piquancy to "displaying oneself," as Marie-Gisèle put it, to the world at large without the muting presence of husbands. And as they left Marie-Gisèle was still in a mischievous mood. "There is Jean!" And so he was, leaning against the broom with which he had swept the veranda and inhaling a cigarette. "Let us ask him!"

"Ask him what?"

"Why about the Calvets, and Gilbert . . . who knows more about people than a hall porter?" And, laughing, they surrounded him, leaning upon the porch rail. *"Tiens, mesdames,"* he said amicably, "and what are you doing to Jean now?"

"It is the other way about: we want you to tell us where we can find those handsome young men, Gilbert and Mathieu, to take us to lunch!"

"Ah, ceux-là! They would do it in an instant, but I am afraid they will be engaged already. Never have I seen two young men more industrious in the pursuit of pleasure—my friends tell me they have more lady friends than a sultan! And who can blame them? Vacation comes but once a year, and if they seem to prefer the riper charms, I imagine the pastures are richer there also!"

"And where do they spend their time when not with the ladies? Do they fish? Swim?"

"No, on the beach they do exercises: they are fanatics for

the physical culture. Ah—and tennis! I believe M. Machicoulet enjoys that game: perhaps he is there now, and if you appear . . ."

Marie laughed. "No. If what you say is true, he will be taken by now. And M. Calvet? can we perhaps inveigle the eminent politician?"

"No, madame, I think not. His wife amuses herself, but he —he works: the lunches with the wealthy, the dinners with the prominent. Another industrious one!"

"And why, when he already has his seat in the assembly?"

Jean winked. "For the cabinet, maybe even, eh, *le Chef d'État?* He establishes, as they say in the newspapers, a base of power. For that, one works very hard to become known, to exchange views, to make promises—who knows?"

"And do you think he will succeed?"

"It may be, madame. He has a way of saying a fact so that you perceive at once it is a fact; and when he then deduces the consequences you are not inclined to argue. It is a gift, that, amid so much rhetoric! I tell you, madame, the first tip from him, I put it away in the drawer, thinking, 'Jean, my boy, one day you may be able to say *le Président de la République* gave you that!'"

They lunched in style at the harbor and unapproached by any man; then strolled the quay asking one another in a totally uninformed manner what sort of boat that might be; cooing irresistibly, too, over a cabin cruiser with pale blue curtains. "What a way to live!" mourned Marie-Gisèle, "and what a pity I am seasick! But look—just putting out in the sailboat—isn't that Gilbert Machicoulet, and Mme. Calvet with him?"

They watched silently; her head was flung back, her throat swelled in a beautiful curve of laughter. "Germaine says . . . but at any rate, I suppose they cannot get into much trouble in a boat!"

"I believe, all the same"—Laura was thoughtful—"that she is totally devoted to her husband."

"Yes? But that could be just the reason."

"How?"

"Well, it cannot be very amusing for her: always on show, always in his shadow. And for some of us that is the only way we can imagine to escape for a while: a new man, a new image."

"Do you feel like that?" Laura was surprised, curious.

"Oh yes, once in a while. Our life is Marc's, his job, his progress—I am only, so to speak, the supporting pillar. Whereas for a lover, it would be *you* who was important: how frivolous, how delightful one might become if one were, even for a few weeks, in the limelight . . . Have you ever had an affair, Laura?"

Laura was yet more surprised; Marie-Gisèle asked the question casually, without embarrassment, as if it were the sort of thing women always talked about. And perhaps it was: motherless at twelve, oriented to male companionship, she had been singularly deprived of women friends. "No," she said amused, "my instinct is always to be monogamous—as long as the marriage lasts, that is!" Yet she could not, now, imagine a future in which this marriage would change, in which François, Franchot, and herself would not be an imperishable trinity, in comparison to which the lives of all these holiday companions, indeed the life and death of Edith Lemay herself, were passing shadows.

Lying in bed that night, François's finger tracing the curve of her breast and the night Atlantic breeze from the window doing the same—one of those serendipities which only occur on holiday in a strange place—François said suddenly, "Is it a bore for you that we are on holiday with Marc and Marie instead of by ourselves?" It was one of those questions that from time to time moved her heart unbearably toward him: a child suddenly seeking reassurance from within the self-sufficiency of the adult. Just such a question: "Laura?" had broken through her defenses, her hesitations, when Paul had been dead fifteen months—"No, of course not!" turning toward him. "Marie-Gisèle is very good company, we had a woman's lunch, flirted with Jean, and amused ourselves enormously! Oh, and François, in the morning I took the necklace to a jeweler for appraisal; Sarrazin told me the name of a good one, and we should have a figure on it by Thursday."

He frowned, and she thought suddenly, I should not have done that without asking. But he only said, "Good. We may need to know what its value is fairly soon, perhaps—you know Marc talked to Jouvet, who said the *juge d'instruction* does not want Leclerc arrested without more evidence—*and* he is very interested in your jewel thief. So after all it may end quite simply . . . But you are quite sure that you are enjoying the holiday? I lived, you know, a long time alone, and it's an old habit to decide things without asking . . . It doesn't annoy you that Marie-Gisèle thinks Romanesque churches resemble dollhouses?"

It was not exactly what Marie-Gisèle had said, but it captured the truth more exactly, and she laughed. "Why, when it is just what I think myself—a small world of its own, safe, quiet, impregnable?"

"Like ours," he said gently and, folded together, they slept in the silence.

CHAPTER 18

But, next morning, tranquillity was suddenly shattered. As they sat over breakfast, Jouvet and Sarrazin appeared in the hall, said a word to madame, and mounted the stairs rapidly. There were cries, the sound of a chair going over; and when they descended Gilbert and Mathieu, in handcuffs, went before them.

Behind came the Calvets, and he was expostulating; she, distraught but stubborn. "No, Jean, you *cannot* go with me. If a photographer—a reporter . . ."

"But you must, I insist. Someone must go with you—a lawyer . . ." He caught sight of François in the doorway. "M. LeBreton . . ."

"No!" It was almost hysterical. "If I must have someone, let it be a woman . . . Mme. LeBreton, will *you* come with me to the Préfecture?"

"Certainly. Just let me get a sweater."

Sarrazin drove like a demon, and Mme. Calvet clutched Laura's hand, impulsively. She held it; then, shifting, put one arm about her hunched shoulders. She did not know why this woman was suffering, but she was a woman and in trouble: that was enough. At the Préfecture Jouvet greeted them, calling over his shoulder, "Sarrazin, search that room carefully!" and ushered Mme. Calvet to a chair. She looked about the room fearfully; it seemed crowded: Jouvet's bulk, the *juge d'instruction*, a man in his fifties in gray hair and gray suit, and his *greffier*. "It would be easier, we thought, madame, for you to tell your story only once, to all of us. Would you, then, mind repeating what you said at eight this morning over the telephone?"

She looked about her, hunted; and Laura, sitting back of her against the wall, wished she were closer. "Tell me first . . . is it absolutely necessary that any of this be made public? The newspapers . . . you can imagine!"

The *juge* cleared his throat; obviously, for the wife of Jean Calvet, any precaution possible would be taken. "Madame, we cannot charge these men without your evidence. And later, it may be, if there is a trial you will have to witness. However . . ." he looked at Jouvet, "the commissioner tells me that he is sure these men are wanted for other offenses. If so, it may be possible to convict them without calling you . . . What we can do, we will—but now, it is but to repeat what you have already told us."

She shook her head, but more in despair than denial. "Must I say—must I say everything?"

"You must say how the robbery occurred, yes, madame."

She drew a deep breath. "Then—you know that we are on holiday."

"Yes, madame."

"And that my husband"—she searched for words—"has, even on holiday, many things to do. People to see, meetings to visit, places to go where my presence might not be suitable."

The magistrate inclined his head, "Of course, madame."

"It is always so. And so . . . it is *normal* for me to keep other company, to go out when he is busy, with friends, but also at times with a cousin, a male acquaintance . . ."

"Yes, yes." Jouvet. "We may live in the provinces, madame, but we are not quite antediluvian!"

She gave him a faint smile, and glanced at the *greffier*, scribbling away. "But this is not testimony, you understand; I only want to explain how it was that . . ."

"You met M. Machicoulet."

"Yes . . . I did not know him before, of course; but he was in the same pension, it was a family hotel, very respectable, and his manners were excellent. I talked to him first about tennis. I wanted to play and he also . . ."

"Naturally."

"So when we fell in with one another again, and he offered coffee, I did not . . . He was entertaining and quite correct! We played tennis again, went for a cognac one evening, and just yesterday, he took me sailing . . ."

The magistrate intervened. "And there was nothing in his manner to make you think . . . ?"

She hesitated; she is going to lie, Laura thought, and I don't blame her. But she did not; she drew a deep breath and said firmly, "No, I cannot say that . . . In retrospect . . . There was a tendency, I must confess to you, to . . . flirt. To flirt, nothing more! But there are those who flirt as they breathe, we were here only for a short time, and knowing who I was I thought that he . . ."

"She could hardly," said Laura from the back of the room, "tell him to go away without making *too* much of it!"

Mme. Calvet looked back at her gratefully. "Mme. LeBreton puts it well . . . though she is much too kind to me. I was abominably, incredibly stupid—Caesar's wife, if I had only remembered that! And so last night . . . oh, how can I possibly say it in words?"

The magistrate looked upon her magisterially, but not unkindly. "Use whatever terms are easiest, madame. He came to your room, did he not?"

"He came into my room . . . I was terrified, I did not know what to think. His attitude was . . . of course I expected him! I had told him my husband would be out, had I not? 'What was that if not invitation?' And I was already in bed, you see." Her tone was submissive, frightened, a supplication; Laura understood her if the men did not.

"Did you cry out? Could someone have come to your aid? Did you think of that?" It had to be asked, Jouvet's tone said, for the record.

"No, I was afraid, I tell you! And if they had come . . . he could have said what he pleased! there would still have been scandal! I only tried to persuade him . . ."

"He was, then . . . persuadable!"

"No . . . no! Not at first!" She shut her eyes. "There were certain . . . caresses . . . And he was strong, it took all my strength to get out of the bed, to get to the door, to say that unless he went at once I *would* scream. And he saw that I meant it."

"And then what happened? Tell us as carefully as you can; he did not leave at once, I take it."

"No . . . He was by the bed. My emerald ring, the one my husband had given me, was on the night table. He . . . snarled. Yes," she said wondering, "that is exactly what he did —he snarled. And he snatched it. 'You are a tease,' he said, 'a slut on the outside, but as soon as one touches you, frigid. Well, I will have something at least for my trouble'—and he held up the ring—'Tell your husband you lost it . . . tell him anything else, and I will have things to say too—that I had you, and this was your gratitude!' And at that moment I did not dare—if only I could lock the door behind him!"

Three sighs, Laura's, the magistrate's, Jouvet's: the *greffier* was too busy writing to know what he was hearing. "And then, madame. You did not telephone us till this morning. Explanations will be required. Courage! The worst is over."

Yet it scarcely seemed so, perhaps, to Mme. Calvet. "I did not know what to do! To you, I expect, it seems simple, but at that moment . . . *J'étais complètement enervée*, I wept . . ." Tears flowed again, remembering. "I envisioned horrible things. My husband assailing him, headlines in the newspapers: 'Calvet Attacks Wife's Lover: Whose Is the Ring?' Abominable! And for all it was my favorite ring, it was insured, it might be worth it, perhaps, to pay the cost and say nothing . . ."

"The American lady," Laura murmured to Jouvet, and he nodded. "Others have thought so before you, madame . . . but you, bravely, spoke in the end. How did that come about?"

"My husband came home, and"—she bowed her head, shrank into herself—"he touched me. Oh!"—the head went up suddenly—"I cannot expect you to understand, but I have never lied to him, never, never been touched by . . . Those other touches, I could not forget they were there, they were like—filth, stains! So he saw at once that something was wrong and would not let me be till I told him . . . He insisted, then, that I report it; but the hall phone, with that man upstairs, perhaps hearing . . . and everything else was closed, of course. We did not sleep at all, and as soon as it was light, we called you."

Now, truly, it was over; the magistrate turned to his clerk; there was a knock on the door and Jouvet opened it. It was Sarrazin. "Sorry to disturb you, chief, but I thought you should know . . . in that room, a real haul! Not only Mme. Calvet's emerald, but the ruby that belonged to the American lady, and . . . among other things . . . a diamond ring and a pin which, we hope, can soon be identified as the property of one Edith Lemay, recently assassinated."

"And you believed her?"

Marc's tone was not critical, but curious; they were sitting on the banks of the Gironde, eating a late picnic lunch Marie-Gisèle had provided. For, during the morning, they had all been sufficiently occupied; François had had an excitable Jacques Leclerc on his hands demanding to know what all this meant, was he now vindicated? Marc had had, after all, to go down to the Préfecture with Jean Calvet to reclaim his wife, and Jouvet had kept him a full half-hour, chortling at the pleasure of capturing not one, but two jewel thieves the PJ itself had vainly wanted, and rubbing it in not a little! And Marie-Gisèle now said energetically, "Of course she believed her—what woman would make up a tale like that if there was no truth in it?"

Laura bit the end off her crisp baguette, considering. "Yes, I believed her." Not entirely; Mme. Calvet had enjoyed her flirtation—no woman of nearly thirty could be quite so naive as that. But at the end, her statement that she could not let her husband touch her without confessing . . . that had carried absolute conviction. Had not Laura herself, for more than a year, shunned François's touch—not only because those were the hands that had killed her husband but because, having passed through too many other and dishonest hands, she had felt herself irretrievably soiled, untrustworthy, stupid . . . unworthy? Only the realization of what this was doing to *François* had enabled her, at the last, to overcome it. And if that was true, the rest was true also. She said so."

"But Machicoulet denies it." Marc was musing, half-unbelieving. "*He* says that she came to *his* room, that there were certain passages . . . and that she was the aggressor, but nothing happened!"

A duet of female laughter. "Gilbert? And nothing happened?" Marie-Gisèle. "*À d'autres!*"

"No doubt you are right." François, slicing the saucisson, handed a piece to Laura. "Which makes Mme. Calvet's story all the more believable. I only wonder why she decided to tell it. People like that, you know—one would think Calvet would be as anxious to hush it up as she was."

"Eh—perhaps he is truly an honest man!"—though Marc was reluctant to think it of an industrialist, much less of a politician. "But there is no doubt really, you know. They worked as a team, the pair of them—a week or so here and then on to the next resort—between them they could fleece any woman worth fleecing. Smooth seduction, a night of love lurid enough the woman would be ashamed to talk about it afterward, and a quick flit with the jewelry. Maybe, too, they went in for a little blackmail after! A neat set-up; I'm really not surprised it took us so long to catch up with them."

"Especially as"—Marie-Gisèle was well-informed here—"the wanted flyer only mentioned *one* thief."

"Yes, Jouvet said he was relieved to discover no one male could perform such a marathon! But it was an advantage perhaps, that they looked roughly alike—it could confuse identification, they could give one another an alibi . . . they are in fact cousins."

"Odd, though"—François had a lawyer's technical curiosity—"that in that case they did not set up an alibi for the night of Edith Lemay's death. They do not even say they were together, you tell me—and each is looking at the other very suspiciously."

"An impulse on someone's part!" Marc waved a hand. "And then—whoever it was was afraid to tell his partner. It might have looked perhaps like a double-cross? But we shall get them both, never fear, before we are finished, for one thing or the other. And it was in Gilbert's drawer, separate from the other jewelry, that Mme. Calvet's emerald and Mme. Lemay's stuff was found."

"Lying about like that?" Laura was disbelieving. "And the rest, was it hidden?"

"Oh yes—in the toilet tank—they had read a *roman policier* sometime!" Marc snorted. "Slick enough, but not really professional for all that—if you're a pro, you package your loot up, mail it *Poste restante* to the next place you're going, and pick it up later . . . And that, no doubt, is why Edith Lemay was killed—a not-quite-professional trying something new and panicking."

An easy gloss, and Marc and François seemed fairly satisfied with it—but Laura, munching her *saucisson* sandwich, was troubled. No previous history of violence; a quite different modus operandi. No effort to hide the ring, the pin, though they were damaging evidence of murder. No weapon, which Jouvet had once thought it so important to identify. And, most disturbing of all, they had only arrived in Royan a few hours before Edith Lemay died.

Of course, one could make a case—and it might even include that crucial moment before the villa. Edith Lemay had already, somewhere else, been their victim; seeing them, she had staggered back and, telephoning Jean, sought their names in order to be able to report them. But they, outguessing her, had learned her address, armed themselves, and killed her hastily even before darkness descended. A perfect case: only—she had never learned their names, and

Laura was absolutely certain they had not seen her. Two dark heads, upraised, waiting for Germaine and Michel to descend the steps; then they had gone in—and she herself had never seen their faces.

Moreover, they denied it. The only evidence was the ring, the pin, for all that was enough to hang them. Think about that, then. How, if they had not killed Edith Lemay, had her jewels arrived in Gilbert's bureau? Just suppose—there was someone in the house burdened with ring and pin, taken to simulate a robbery; unable to throw them away in case they were found, unable to sell them for fear of identification; yet knowing all the same they were damning evidence. The turmoil this morning—an opportunity. Gilbert and Mathieu arrested, their room perhaps empty and open—or if locked, all the rooms in the villa had skeleton keys, and she was willing to bet what fit one would fit another. Two seconds, in and out, before Sarrazin returned for the searching . . .

But one would have to know, or guess, what kind of men these were. Criminals, of course, but a little more, surely? If the police found jewels in the room of a forger, an income tax evader, would they not be a bit puzzled?

Who might guess?

Jacques Leclerc, who was a journalist, who must have seen criminals often. Who came from Marseille, not far from beach resorts where they might already have operated. Who had, at that moment, a very powerful motive to pin the crime on another person.

Germaine Moreuil: was it not she who had told Laura of seeing Mathieu with an older woman? She and Michel: he had been at the jazz bar too. And they, like the Leclercs, had rooms on the same floor as the jewel thieves.

But, most obviously of all, Jean Calvet, who knew even before the police took them away exactly what sort of men they were, and who would have a strong emotional as well as a practical reason to fix the blame for Edith Lemay's death on them.

But if it had been done that way, it had been done by somebody at the villa.

At supper that night the Calvets were conspicuously absent, but everyone else was only too obvious. The Leclercs with Jacquot, she arrogantly beaming, he, though he made no great show of it, ordering champagne with their dinner. The Moreuils: Michel, limping wearily and leaning on the thick curved-headed cane which Germaine had said he hated, made a point of wishing a cordial good evening to the Leclerc table; Germaine did not. And the Antonionis! It had just come to their ears, apparently, that they were taking their holidays in the midst of a murder mystery, and papa and son-in-law were explaining it all to them. A great deal of Italian, and then *"il nipote."* Simultaneously thirteen pairs of eyes, unabashed, piercing and not unfriendly, focused on Jacques Leclerc. More Italian, and *"l'avvocato di Parigi."* Thirteen heads swiveled to study François's appearance. More Italian and *"la gioielleria."* Thirteen faces, those of the women more speculative this time, fixed upon Laura. It was amusing, but it was also embarrassing, and they fled to the salon, following the Moreuils, as soon as possible.

But their embarrassments had not ended. Jacques Leclerc, Yvonne behind him, descended upon them. "M. LeBreton! *Mon cher maître!"* Willy-nilly, and it was nilly, he kissed François on both cheeks ceremoniously. "A happy outcome of our tribulations, eh? Jewel thieves—and my aunt's jewelry in their possession—do I guess correctly? But now, tell me—is it possible, do you think, for me to see your friend the commissioner? Ah, what a story! And I deserve it, do I not? Don't you think that *I* am owed something?"

François, for once, was speechless. "Well, you can try, I suppose!" said Marc, amused. "You know where to find the Préfecture—and the telephone!"

"So I shall certainly do!" Not in the least discouraged, he took the table by the window where the Calvets had sat and raised a finger. "Jean! Your best Armagnac!"

Yvonne Leclerc glanced after him but did not follow: it was the cost, not the consumption, of Armagnac which apparently concerned her. "Now, M. LeBreton, that it is clear Jacques is innocent, the inheritance—when will we be able to draw on it? Soon, surely?"

François hemmed and hawed exactly, Laura thought, like a lawyer. There were formalities. They must be completed. In the estate there was almost no liquid funds; it would take time before the house was sold . . .

"And her other jewels! The emerald necklace!" Balked, she was furious. "One could sell that tomorrow!"

"The other jewels are impounded as material evidence. As for the necklace . . ."

"I have taken it to be appraised, madame," said Laura. "It will have to be valued, of course, before . . ."

Yvonne Leclerc turned on her. "Ah, you have your hands on it! I might have known! Tell me," to François, "is that your idea? To have your wife cheat us out of it?"

"In fact," said François in measured terms, "it was left to her in the will, but . . ."

"I do not claim it." The interjection was Laura's. "No, Mme. Leclerc, I do not claim it and I do not think I have any right to it. But you must understand that everything is not clear yet, that we do not know whether . . ." Whether it is evidence of a sort, she would have said, but Yvonne Leclerc leaped to other conclusions.

"You doubt Jacques still perhaps! Or perhaps it is me, now —anything to keep it to yourself, out of the hands of its rightful owners!"

They all exclaimed, but it was Germaine Moreuil who most effectively came to Laura's defense. She turned in her chair and said in commanding tones, "Mme. Leclerc! This will not do, you know. They are quite right, there are many formalities and you would do well to accept them or in fact people may wonder."

Yvonne Leclerc subsided, considering this, but only for an instant; then she passed to the counterattack. "Ah, they may wonder, madame? And while they are wondering may they not wonder about you, and your sainted husband? Who knew Madame Lemay so *well*—oh yes, I am not quite stupid!—and who sits meekly there with his little cane with the lead in the handle? I . . ."

Germaine Moreuil rose, majestic, calm, and—as Laura suddenly realized—totally out of control. "You little bitch," she said. "Oh, you are not so much of a bitch as your aunt-in-law, but I am getting very tired of you too. Go to your room at once." And a stunned audience beheld the spectacle of a woman of sixty-seven dispassionately striking a woman of thirty across the face so hard that white showed on her cheekbone.

And then the spectacle of an old man of seventy-five, his own countenance pale as parchment, eyes cold, face averted in total rejection, walk past his wife without looking at her and slowly go up the stairs.

Germaine put a hand to her mouth, choked out a sound, and ran through the front door. There was a moment's shocked silence, then François said to Laura, "Go after her."

She found her in the garden, weeping beneath a laburnum, and when she saw her, Germaine flung out a hand wildly—appeal or rejection—and then turned her face to the tree trunk. "He hates me! Ever since she died, he has hated me, and he has reason—he grieves, and I say hateful things; but seeing him grieve, how can I help it?" Sobs strangled her. "He grieves his whole life gone, and I am not even in it!"

Laura could find nothing to say to her, only, "Germaine—it was a long time ago."

"Well? You are not one of those people who think when one turns sixty one suddenly becomes of marble, are you? When you were a little girl punished for something you didn't do—have you forgotten? Is she still not alive in you?"

Laura's hand went to her cheek, involuntary; the analogy had struck home. The slap was still as sharp, the surprise as heartbreaking, as if it were yesterday. "Think," Germaine Moreuil turned to her, her face blotched, her lip trembling,

"I was twenty-six when I married him, knowing I was his second choice. You don't think that hurt, then? And some hurts don't change, you just forget them for longer and longer . . . And sometimes I think when you remember it's bitterer—one year, five, ten—because one year, five, ten have gone and nothing is different.

"I have always taken second place in his life—third, fourth! Her first; then his work, then the children . . ." And so much for Marie's theory, thought Laura. "Oh, *va pour les enfants*. They were part mine, anyway, when he loved them he loved me . . . if she had borne *him* a child I would have killed her then, I think. But how do you compete with a dream, with his youth—with a woman who doesn't really exist, who is just out there on a stage someplace singing sad songs? It's not fair, it's not fair—I have deserved better than that!"

Laura put her arms about her and felt that tall full woman melt against her as if she were a child. "There," she said, "there . . . Of course you have. But now, Germaine . . . now, if you can only let go of her . . . perhaps he will too."

CHAPTER 19

Laura woke the next morning in a bad temper. Last night's display of bitternesses still rankled; and, while she had still been busy comforting Germaine Moreuil, François had had the nerve to call Montargis without her and report back that Franchot had a runny nose, but it was nothing! She did not like having only four days of holiday left when François was just starting to relax and the affair of Edith Lemay was not settled to her satisfaction. She did not like having four long days of holiday left when Franchot had a runny nose and perhaps needed a mother. Torn in two directions, she sat up, wriggled her toes, and said, "I feel bitchy."

"*Vrai?* Then you had better run around the block," said François tranquilly.

She laughed. She had confessed to him once that when she was married to Harry, and his drinking—or rather what it was doing to him—became too much for her, she would leave their New York apartment in the middle of the night and run round and round the block looking for a mugger so that she could *kill* him! That he remembered made her feel comforted, cherished. "Well, so I will!" and she got up and began to dress.

"What will you do?"

"Take a run on the beach, meet you for breakfast, and"—what one jewel proved another might alter—"take the car to Royan and find out what my jeweler has to say about the emerald necklace."

"And I shall lie on the beach."

"Very well—but don't forget, we decided to take the boat

trip up the Charente yesterday . . . and someone should find out when it leaves and where!"

"Yes, yes, good wife!" He buried his head again in the pillow.

So it was with the sense of doing at least one thing useful that she entered the jeweler's shop when it opened at ten. She had still to wait fifteen minutes for M. Pierre, but his brisk expression when he emerged from the shop's little office made her feel hopeful. "Yes indeed, madame, I have accomplished your miracle for you! It was created . . . I say created advisably, because it is truly exquisite . . . in 1935 by"—he named a name no doubt worthy of the reverence he paid it, but to Laura totally unmemorable—"for a gentleman from Poitiers by the name of Christophe Calvet. And," he unfolded its tissue paper tenderly, "I have set a value on it which may perhaps surprise you."

The figure on the folded letterhead beneath the necklace did surprise her, but not much: another astonishment had left no room for it. "Christophe Calvet! Are you quite certain?"

"Oh yes, madame. It is a responsible firm, and their records are impeccable. You understand, with important pieces, there may be at any time a question of valuation, of ownership . . . and of course there is supporting evidence for this identification. The initials we observed in the setting . . . the other one is quite definitely, both when one looks at it and in the original description, a *C*."

Breathless, she burst into their room at the villa where François was just changing out of his trunks. "François! Do you know that the necklace is worth more than half a million francs? And do you know who gave it to her? Christophe Calvet!"

François stared at her. "Half a million . . . What have you done with it?"

"Left it in the jeweler's safe, for the moment. Insured . . .

But don't you think it's curious—significant, maybe—that it was the gift of a Calvet, probably Jean Calvet's father?"

For a moment his gaze focused. "You don't know that—and in any case, I assure you, they could have no possible legal claim to it! But . . . half a million? And how are we to get it back to Paris, I ask you?—Oh, the boat leaves at noon; you had better hurry!"

"Are you ready yet?" Marie-Gisèle's voice accompanied her rap on the door, and there was no time left for anything but scrambling.

They barely made the boat, a pleasantly ancient white vessel with colorful awnings, benches on deck, and a small wheelhouse-cum-bar where passengers could if it rained huddle and befuddle themselves. Scarcely had they taken their seats when the motor started, and Marie-Gisèle clutched Marc's hand. "Oh! Why am I doing this? We forgot —I get seasick!" It was indeed an ill-conceived expedition, for it soon emerged that no one had thought how they were to get back again . . .

A brief conference over the schedule posted on the wheel-house, however, indicated that once arrived in Cognac, they could take the boat back to Saintes an hour and a half later. "And there may also be buses or trains," Laura pointed out. "Dull, certainly"—this was François—"to go back as we came —we shall have to sit on one side this trip, and on the other the other!" Marie-Gisèle, looking pale, said nothing . . . The truth was, thought Laura, they had arrived at the point in their holiday when each would individually have pre-ferred to do something different, and the boat trip had been snatched at because no one had any other ideas. No doubt each of them would be cross—cross at himself for failing to plan better—and she must keep a good eye on her own temper!

But the voyage was in fact soothing. As the water drifted silently under the hull, the aroma of vermouth and Coca-Cola scented the air, and small children clung to the rails cooing only to be snatched away by their anxious mothers, insensibly the strain eased and the spirit abandoned its inner stress to float outward into the landscape. "C'est joli," said Marie-Gisèle gratefully, loosening her handclasp on Marc, and it was. The gentle light, pervading the faintest of mists, caressed the low hills in a pearly radiance; from blue slopes to bronzy green vineyards to pale river, the scoped vista displayed all the tints of a Corot in watercolor. "Those are the grapes of cognac," observed Marc with satisfaction, and François, with enthusiasm, "And at Cognac we shall soon taste them!"

"Ah bon, bon," observed the sturdy middle-aged man, face ruddy under a gray stubble, who sat on the bench opposite them. "And you will visit a distillery, perhaps, when you are in Cognac? To see the grape become the ambrosia? No? your boat gives you no time for that, and your car is at Saintes? Hm, hm. Well, supposing I give you this tour, and run you back afterward? Would that be agreeable?"

They were all taken aback, and he laughed jovially. "Oh, you can get tickets for the tour at the Bureau de Tourisme, hours from 9 to 11, 2 to 4:30—but I am offering you something better than that—a free tour with an expert."

It intrigued them, but . . . "Do we then—return the favor in some way?" inquired François delicately. Ticket scalpers were not unknown in the theater, but in a distillery . . . ? The stranger's laugh this time was rich, conspiratorial. "Not a sou, only the pleasure of showing charming strangers my own business . . . Yes, I am a distillery owner, or part owner, retired—Hutin, at your service." He proffered a card. "And the old man having been kicked upstairs to the board of directors, he has nothing better to do on a fine morning than float up and down his river and reflect on its history . . . My plant is near the *quais*, handy for shipping, though most of it is by rail nowadays . . . But in the old times, ah, this was a busy waterway! not only the cognac, but lumber, fish, salt from the marshes . . . No doubt my Celtic ancestors plied this route, and my Roman too, if I had any, on their way to Mediolanum Santonum . . . The making of wine, of course, is as old as the grape, or nearly . . . *un sacré breuvage* in both senses of the word, the liquor that makes you a god, or a demon! But cognac, alas, has not so ancient a history, the burnt wine, brandevin, comes later."

"When?" Laura wanted to know.

"About the seventeenth century, Madame Laura LeBreton—oh yes, you used first names, I read the papers and I recognized you. And I said to myself, 'These intelligent people will take an interest . . . besides, I may need an eminent Paris lawyer one of these days!'" He chuckled and would have dug François in the ribs could he have reached them. "A great invention, the brandy. And you can see its advantage to us—only one small cask to ship instead of seven of wine, and keeping much longer . . . But we arrive. This way!"

It was impossible to say no to him, nor did they really want to. And so they spent the heat of the afternoon in his cool chais, admiring the immense hammered copper alembic vessels in which the wine underwent its first gentle shrinkage by open fire, its second twelve-hour cooking in the vast kettles from which, rising through the "swan's neck" and descending through the "serpentine," its essence warmed, cooled, condensed, and became raw brandy. Trotting merrily through the plant on his thick legs, offering here a "Bonjour, Jean," there a "Comment ça va?" their guide was obviously enjoying himself immensely and, threading them through the vast cellars where the cognac aged, took on color and flavor from the oaken barrels of Limousin, he insisted on "trying their palate" with one sample after another. So that when they staggered out into the light of day it stunned like an arc of heat lightning, and Marie-Gisèle, turning a color that could only be described as celadon, exclaimed faintly and staggered. "Oh! I am going to be sick."

"Hup! Ho!" said their host in alarm. "Try to hold on five minutes . . . we shall go home to my wife, she will take care of that!"

Even at top speed it was more like fifteen than five, and

when Marie-Gisèle stumbled into their benefactor's hall, his
wife took one look at her clammy face and flung an indica-
tory arm toward the staircase. Laura followed them, and
Mme. Hutin set Marie down on the bed, taking her shoes off
and seizing a bathroom washcloth to put to her head . . .
Laura looked about the room: white bamboo, and the bamboo pattern repeated in green and buttercup on the curtains;
what she had seen of the downstairs was Swedish modern,
blond wood and immense white sofas—certainly their hosts
were prosperous!

Apologetically, enjoying the coolness of the dim room, she
explained to their hostess who they were and how they came
to be in her bedroom. "And no lunch either, I suppose!" It
was now after three. She went to the door and called, a
vigorous hog call, "Mi-che-lle! A cold collation. And no wine!
—some Perrier, it is good for the stomach. Ah, these men!"
Her vigor was a west wind that rejoices in its own energy.
"These men—we bring them up wrong, you know. Work, we
say. Get to the top of the tree—it is a greased pole, you know,
but we don't say so. And when they get to the top, what can
they do then but sit on it? It is not amusing, *vous savez*, to sit
on the top of a pole; of course they can stand on their heads
on it, which is what he is doing now, *mais enfin* . . . Work in
the garden, I say. Join the Rotary and make interesting acquaintances . . . but no, he will not do that. Travel, I would
like to see Spain, but no he says they don't talk French there
and the coffee is frightful. All he cares to do still is tinker with
that business of his, make it run even better . . . Well, at
least he gets out of the house and does not stay under my feet
all day!—It goes better, *ma petite?*"

"A little." Marie-Gisèle groaned, but only faintly. "My
stomach has settled . . . only the dizziness . . ."

"Well, that is no food—And your husbands, what were they
about to let you get into this state?—you have sons, mesdames?" They agreed that they did. "Well, for the love of
God, raise them to have some consideration. Teach them to
smell the flowers, to look at the sky, to realize that women

have feelings. This may not at first seem very important, but past forty-five if they have not the right training they are capable of any folly."

And, when they at last descended to a cool dining room where a cold meat plate and salad and Perrier had been set out for them, she berated her husband soundly. *"Ah, vrai"*— he expressed an instant's repentance—"but just think, my dear—these gentlemen have met Jean Calvet, he stays in Pontaillac at the same villa!"

Her sniff was eloquent, but his interest was not so easily diverted. "Ah, that Calvet! Produce! he says, and you will become rich! Well, it cannot be argued against. All these high-faluting economic theories, but it always comes down to that: the less we produce, the poorer we are. And this social-ist government, what it comes down to is putting more bu-reaucrats, more paperasses, in the way of production!"

"Well, I am not so sure," said Marc smiling—his political views confined themselves to who meddled with the police and who did not—"produce, all very well; but who is to receive the fruits of production, and in what proportion— that is an equally difficult question, is it not?"

They fell into amiable argument, and Mme. Hutin urged Marie-Gisèle to more Perrier. "He is *toqué* about politics now too," she confided to Laura, "pure waste of time, if you ask me. And Jean Calvet, well, that is a prime example of what I was telling you . . . Why, of not being properly brought up! Always climbing the greased pole: first it was learning to run the factory, night and day like my Hutin, and now it is poli-tics. Much too busy to marry, of course! and then when he does, in his forties, who does he pick but a girl twenty years younger, not a countess, not even a proper bourgeoise, but a girl who was waitress in a cabaret where the serving staff danced with the customers!"

Marie-Gisèle choked in surprise, and Mme. Hutin nodded wisely. "Oh, they do not mention that now; but I know—I am from Poitiers, *vous savez*. Of course it was not such a bad place really; my uncle had the *tabac* next door. But he could have had anyone: much better for him if he had chased the girls like his father and gotten it out of his system."

"And did you know"—Laura crossed her fingers—"his father? Christophe Calvet, was it not?"

"Oh, assuredly, everyone knew M. Christophe—a handsome fellow. I did not know him well, of course—he died early in the war, and I was only a little girl at the time. But Jean was my age, and he took the world just as seriously then as he does now, only he did not talk about it!"

She sat back, satisfied with the impression she had made, but Marie-Gisèle had now recovered from Perrier water up the nose and wanted to know more. "But she has done well, Mme. Calvet, all the same—very elegant, every inch the lady."

"Ah yes, I do not say no, for a girl whose mother was some poor Parisienne on holiday and who never knew who her father was! The Malvoisins, who adopted her, were quite respectable people, too, though he was only a postman. But what I say is, blood will tell, and it sometimes tells some surprising things when you do not know whose blood it is!"

M. Hutin, as good as his word, drove them back to Saintes; but Marie-Gisèle, now perfectly recovered, did not want to go home at once. "You know, the villa is a charming place, but more and more I wonder there what is going to jump out at me next! I would like to walk the streets, look in all the shop windows, then eat a tremendous meal at some little bistro by the river where you can watch the anglers dangle!" It appealed to all of them; and the restaurant they finally found was peaceful and empty except for a handsome man in his seventies, white-suited and panama-hatted in the style of Maurice Chevalier, who brooded over his glass as if it encompassed not only the Charente but all the world's oceans . . . The food was good, and they could talk at leisure: and Laura told them the life story of Edith Lemay as reflected by Michel Moreuil and the emerald necklace. "And that," she concluded, "was the message she meant to send me—Christophe Calvet—an *E* and a *C* intertwined. But what it means I still don't know—except that it draws more parallels . . ." Parallels, that was the word to link some of the thoughts churning in her mind; if she could only hold on to it . . .

"Parallels?" Marc cocked an eyebrow, dubious but interested.

"Two jewel thieves." She sorted them out on her fingers, "Two generations of Calvets. Two links with Poitiers—the Calvets, Edith Lemay and Robert's father. Her career: twice she nearly made it to the top, both times something happened. Two rings: Edith Lemay's, Jeanne Calvet's . . ."

"Yes," said Marie-Gisèle, suddenly joining the game, "and two emeralds, the ring and the necklace!"

"Yes." Laura looked at her, startled, "maybe that too . . . ! She saw someone at the villa, she called Jean to hear one name, she inscribed her will to François and the necklace to me, clues, that very day—yes, Marc, I am sure that was how it was—and she was killed. If we could only link those things, we would know why . . ."

"Yes, but one finds murderers not by parallels, but by direct lines—and one has already led us there!" Marc was hardheaded. "There is no connection between the Jean Calvets and the necklace—given the circumstances, he would not even have known about it! Your emerald necklace has a missing link, Laura—if indeed it is not a red herring!"

"Worse than a red herring, an albatross," said François gloomily. "Half a million francs . . . how am I to get it back to Paris? If anything happens to it, Yvonne Leclerc will dissect me!"

"Leave it where it is," Marc advised. "Then, when the estate is settled, have the jeweler send it to the heir. He has already insured it—and he will certainly know the best method of transport."

Their host interrupted. "You are satisfied. It was a good dinner. And a liqueur to follow, perhaps." Marie-Gisèle refused, but the rest accepted, and as he served it the white-suited gentleman rose, left some bills on the table, and with a farewell gesture made his way slowly out the door leaning on a cane like Michel Moreuil's. "Eh, *au revoir,* M. Santorini," the innkeeper tossed cordially over his shoulder, and Laura sat up. "You said . . . Santorini?" "Yes, a regular client. Poor fellow, he was in an accident last week. Why does he interest madame?"

"Not unless he wears emerald cuff links, or comes from Poitiers," said Marc amused, sniffing his Benedictine.

Their host laughed. "Poitiers? No. He has lived retired here for several years—his mother came from these parts, you see. But before that—ah, you could probably tell by his dress!—he lived in Paris, where he was a member of the theatrical profession."

CHAPTER 20

A missing link . . . On Friday the holiday link that had kept them one unit dissolved entirely. Marie-Gisèle said that it would be nice to go shopping; Marc said as far as he was concerned it would *not;* and François, who had brought a volume of Thomas Mann with him and sworn to read it, complained he had not even finished the first chapter.

A missing link . . . Laura drove straight as a die to Saintes, in pursuit of a wild gander.

When he opened the door he was not in his white suit: white Dior sweater, skintight jeans, Gucci brogues: a homosexual. And his "Yes?" was not friendly. Well, she would just have to be very American; Americans were detestable no doubt, but less so than plain women. "It is about Edith Lemay," she said brashly, and he did not deny knowledge. "There are things I don't understand at all about her dying, and I thought you could . . ."

"Yes. Well—" He frowned, but not forbiddingly. "I wondered that the police . . . I suppose you are not . . . ?"

"No, I am not official. Laura LeBreton: she left me her emerald necklace."

He looked at her sharply. " 'The affair of the emerald necklace?' Oh come in, come in. My mornings are not, I'm afraid, too amusing these days!"

"No, I am sure they're not! I was surprised to see you mobile—in the newspapers, your accident . . ." He picked up his cane from where he had hidden it behind the door before opening, and hobbled painfully down the hall. "Oh, I am nimble for my age—or I used to be! At first they thought the hip was broken, but it is, it appears, a simple matter of muscles and tendons. Though that is less simple than the hip would have been to cure . . . Doctors, don't you think, are detestable?"

Following him into the morning room, she agreed. It was an interesting den: plants, an old silk oriental on the wall, Kermans and Sarouks on the floor; a divan, Persian prints. He sank into a cushioned rattan chair and she, avoiding the cobra back in which experience had taught her one could never be comfortable, chose a large hassock. To sit suppliant at his knee for knowledge would perhaps have its appeal!

"Achmed! Du café!" he shouted to the back of the house. "And now, Madame LeBreton . . . the notorious Madame Chabre LeBreton, perhaps?"

She agreed, somewhat stiffly, that she was; the Arab boy came with the coffee, and he poured it out. "Hmm . . . and you inquire into the mystery of Edith? I have wondered why no one came to see me, as I was in her address book . . ."

"Her address book was missing; there had been a search as well as a robbery."

"Ah, that explains it." But he was not stupid. "In that case, however, how did *you* find me?"

"Pure coincidence. I saw you at the café last night . . . and an old friend of Edith's who happened to be at the villa where I am staying had already mentioned you. Michel Moreuil?" It was an interrogative, but the name evoked only a headshake; well, perhaps Michel had been telling the truth when he said he had never renewed Edith's acquaintance . . . Or perhaps she had just not said . . . "Is your cane leaded?" she inquired, looking at it curiously.

"No." He looked startled. "But I have another that is . . . we older ones, we must protect ourselves, you know! Look at Edith!"

"You were old friends, I think."

"Oh, friends!" A twist of his mouth deprecated anything as true as friendship. "We had known one another a long time, certainly . . . But what is it you want of me exactly? Did I not read they arrested her murderers yesterday?"

"I wanted . . . to know her better." That was true enough. "I had never met her, you see; but she left me her necklace, and I think she wanted me to understand her . . . So what can you tell me about her life? Did you know Charlie, for instance?"

The name raised his eyebrows, bought partial confidence. "No, I was younger than she by five years, and he was already dead when I met her. I don't even remember now how that came about—No, but I do!" Now that he had begun, the raconteur's pleasure was growing. "A young pianist we both knew, who had played for her in cabarets . . . he took sleeping pills and called us both before he lay down to die! Well, between us we saved him; in time he went back to the provinces where he came from; and she adopted me. She was a great one for adopting people, you know, cooked you up bowls of spaghetti whether you wanted them or not, nagged you to get more exercise . . . I really didn't *need* a mother, my career for that matter was doing much better than hers at that moment. But you know, there is something . . . touching in the sense that someone, however incompatible, cares about you—childish, but irresistible! And she had style—as a producer I could see that, she was an excellent artiste but not quite right for what she was doing. Charisma, they would call it today, that hadn't found its right stage . . ." Curious, it was so close to what Charlie, Michel had said about her.

"So you produced the Girl in the Black Velvet Hat?"

"Oh, not quite right away—and she was scarcely a girl when I got around to it. But we were doing a big revue, American style, at the Casino, and I thought, why not a striptease? It would have to be special, however: something French rather than American; earthy, but some fantasy to it. And I thought suddenly, Edith! She had a magnificent body then, at its absolute peak physically, and that touch of France of 1910 which emanated from her—we could emphasize that, use those marvelous Edwardian costumes. We worked, both of us, like demons, and she pulled it off. Not quite such a hit as when they tore up the Olympia seats for Berthe Sylva —but even Marie Dubas was jealous."

"It made quite an impact, I hear! But—'Vingt Ans de Music Hall'—did you produce that too?"

"Oh yes. She came to me, that time, with the idea, but I saw it instantly. It was exactly the moment, everyone hoping we would have no war, a glance back into peaceful times— but she was unlucky with that too. The Germans came, and she was not of those content to amuse the conquerors—*une vraie Marseillaise,* that one! She joined the Resistance after the surrender."

"I had heard that, but without details . . ."

"Oh yes—courier, agent, in at the drops; she could shoot, our Edith, and who would suspect a middle-aged chanteuse? We even met once, when the General sent me in on liaison, a grateful surprise, I can tell you, to find an old friend helping you out of your harness."

"Then you too . . ."

"Certainly." He grinned, foxlike. "We are not all frail flowers, you know . . ." and he held up a still muscular arm for her inspection. "Besides, the Germans, my dear, not in the least chic, were they?" It was almost a parody, but Laura agreed; it was as good a critique as any.

"But—you said she was always unlucky. What happened after the Girl in the Black Velvet Hat? One would have expected . . . but she dropped out of sight. Was she ill?"

"Not exactly." His tone was sardonic. "Merely pregnant."

"So she did have a child!" Here was a missing link with a vengeance, but the impetuosity with which she greeted it was ill-timed. Santorini withdrew, wary, a man who realizes too late he may have discarded a trump card. "And exactly why is that of importance? If it is a question of legal inheritance, I warn you that I cannot testify . . ."

"Oh no! I don't want the necklace, it's only . . ." But she had made it worse; people who said they did not want emerald necklaces were obviously not to be trusted! In a moment he would ask her to leave—she poured herself a second coffee, territorial claim, and said firmly, "She left it to me, but there is no question of my inheriting. The bequest was made in an unwitnessed codicil, and it will go to her nephew, her heir. I want to know *why* the codicil. She must have known it would not hold water . . . she knew me only by reputation . . . what was it she wanted to tell me? It is that which I hope you will clarify—and I think you know."

He looked at her, calculating; what was his knowledge worth, what benefit could it bring him? And yet, unmistakably curious. "An unwitnessed, last-minute codicil! That sounds like Edith. And—she spoke of you with respect, back when . . . Yes, I think you may be right, she did intend me to tell you. But mind you, there is nothing extraordinary about it—no great scandal, and the child is dead, she once said so." But still he was silent.

"Christophe Calvet is dead too."

"So he is." He paid her unwilling respect. "You *have* done your homework—Well, it was not, even then, much of a secret. When I knew her Edith made no bones about her great ambition: to find a rich man and set herself up for life on the proceeds. But in practice you see," and his sigh hung between affection and exasperation, "she never could stick to it. There was always some penniless lame duck! And when she told me, I supposed . . . I was furious! But no—this time she had made it for real: he was not only rich, but attractive, and I think she was quite fond of him. He wanted the child, she said; only one son, and his wife could have no more children. She showed me the necklace. 'It will be a girl,' she said, 'and this is her dowry.' Yes, frankly, I was impressed for her."

"And was it a girl? What became of her?"

"It was a girl, and I even saw them once on the street together. A quiet charming little thing, not at all like her mother! As for what became of her, pouponnières, I suppose, and then later the child lived with her sister. She was still pursuing her career, you see, hopefully, even though Calvet . . . and I'm sure he made her some sort of allowance . . ."

Exactly. Robert's father's papers—and why had she not

wondered before why the poorer sister was sending money to the richer? But where from here? "And after that? after the war? sometime about 1957, what happened? She went into retreat, became a Protestant, gave up all her old connections?"

He looked surprised. "Was it quite so abrupt as that? We had lost touch, you see. It was not until I retired here, and we met on the street, that . . . Oh, of course her career was finished. She came to see me in '46, and I was quite blunt about it—fighting your country's wars does nothing for your voice or your complexion!"

"How did she take that? Someone so energetic, so ambitious . . ."

"Quite well." He considered. "I think some perspective had changed, for all of us. Before, we had no world but the stage: Ethiopia, Czechoslovakia was irrelevant compared to how many head plumes in this season's revue. Afterward— we knew the tigers at the gate were not papier-mâché, that what we were doing was, after all, transient, fragile. She said that she had started to read, that it was time she repaired her education—she outlined a plan for starting a school for singing and dance. There are always aspirants, you know, who are convinced stardom awaits them, who pride themselves on knowing the difference between *figurante, utilité* and *demi-vedette*—or there used to be. *Demi-vedette!* Edith exactly, half a star, never a whole one."

It was confirmation but no more: not satisfactory. "But there was something more. Something that sent her fleeing to Pontaillac, turned her against the stage, made her a prude —that sent her mad, in fact!"

"She was not mad!" He stood up angrily, pacing and rubbing the thigh: there was more than one sensitivity here. "You misunderstand her. She never turned her back on the stage! Granted we discussed vitamins and *tisanes* most of the time, the stage was what we had in common—the people we talked about. She was a professional and of her theatrical talents she was always, like all professionals, very proud. If there was an abrupt break, as you say, it was some other part of her life which . . ." He sat down again, frowning. "She used to say to me, 'Jules, you have been so good at getting what you want out of life, I'm afraid someday that will make it very difficult to leave it.' I have thought of that often, these last days! She was different, true; quieter . . . I remember her saying once, 'In my youth all I sought was my own will, and the harm that ensued was immense—even now it may be creating havoc somewhere. All I can do to atone is to will to will nothing.' But her dress was not madness. It was, rather, I think, a kind of statement. Had she been a nun, she would have worn the habit. As she was a professional, she wore costume. The costume she chose—it had something to do, I suppose, with memories of her childhood, but that was also an ordered age, elegant, disciplined . . . Obedience to an order: yes, that I think was the logic of what you call her madness."

"I see." She sat back, at last comprehending. "Yes, you have made her very real to me." He was a cold man, this, heart set upon his own pleasures, but in some cranny of his nature he had felt for Edith Lemay a genuine affection. "You understood her very well, I think, and cared about her." He shook his head, impatient; was there a moisture at the corner of his eyes? "Oh yes, all the same—a whole era of your life that vanished with her . . ."

Hands on the arms of his chair he looked at her, sad, defiant . . . "You too—you understand *quite* well, I think . . . And so I will tell you something I had forgotten—She did come to me about the time you mention, very distraught. We were in the midst of rehearsals, two days to opening. Well, I am a selfish man; what was it to me that her daughter was in trouble? She herself had managed very well without my help! . . . I was called away when we had only talked a moment. It was an Arabian number, I remember, we had a camel, it had bitten a stagehand, and they were all threatening to strike if . . . When I came back she had changed her mind. 'You cannot help me, no one can,' she said, and quoted a line, I think from *Phèdre:* surprising, she must have been doing some reading! And she left."

"And did she never talk of it after? Did you never ask her?"

"No. The girl was dead, I supposed in childbirth, and . . . you know, there are questions too dangerous to ask . . . One meets a friend on the street after many years. 'How is your wife?' The wife is dead, and the whole personality collapses. You are right, I was too fond of her to . . . my poor Edith! a life out of time—now if we had only lived in the age when kings had mistresses! We die as we live, they say—well, it was exactly like Edith to get herself murdered. Now I—I will wither away into a heap of dust, they will not even have to cremate me."

"Nonsense," she said robustly: she had quite come to like Jules Santorini. "It is quite clear to me that you are indestructible, especially after your narrow escape last week. You'll see, you will soon be as young as ever . . . Did they ever find the driver who struck you?"

"Oh yes." He grinned, unwillingly. "A Paris taxi driver on holiday!" It was not what she had feared and too pat not to appreciate: for a moment of empathy they laughed together. "You see, even there appropriate! If I am to be run over, it must be by a Parisian! . . . Tell me, have I been of some assistance?"

"Immense." She rose, and he accompanied her to the doorway. "Oh, one more detail—the line from *Phèdre* which she quoted so oddly, can you remember it?"

He considered. "Perhaps. My memory is quite good, you know, especially in what concerns the theater. Oh yes . . ." and his deep voice was still expressive, moving, "it was her line to Oenone, you know, before the confession: *'Tu fremiras d'horreur si je romps le silence.'* Melodramatic, you see, as always!"

CHAPTER 21

"You would tremble with horror, were I to speak . . ." Five miles out of Saintes, she stopped the car and threw up amid columbines and daisies. It was shock; she had done that once before, when the death in question had been her own . . . but this time she was only the gravedigger, pursuing the scent of treasure to the charnelhouse in which it was still buried. Abruptly now all the parallels came into focus: two names, two profiles, two generations, two rings: even, as Marie-Gisèle had suggested, two emeralds.

No—impossible! And yet: Edith Lemay staggering back, calling the villa for the names of the residents, the abrupt gift of an emerald necklace, the naming of François executor, the ring in Gilbert's room: all the bright images now snapped together, flashes of tawny through the leaves that told you even in a quiet beach resort somewhere a lion might lie hidden . . .

Ah, that poor woman! She understood now Edith Lemay whole, as she had not been able to do before. The energy, the ambition, pushing past normal limits, the more determined the more it was thwarted, and then . . . The destruction of hubris: that photograph of The Girl in the Black Velvet Hat not vanity, but the hairshirt of repentance . . . Yet not enough, too dark the incalculable results of sin to be forgiven; a shielding armor, then, of clothes of another age, a time when nothing had yet happened, when there was nothing irrevocable in the life of Edith Lemay . . . Well, she was dead now, *la fille de Minos et de Pasiphaé:* surely that at last was atonement.

But what to do now? The same coincidence twice—who

would believe it? None of this was in any legal sense provable —even the birth records might not . . . Who would have known? Not Christophe Calvet, he died too early. The notary of Poitiers, Robert's father—and he was dead, leaving no meaningful papers behind him. Edith Lemay, and she was now dead—because she had known? Two more? Or one? Or three? Jacques Leclerc perhaps . . . which would have given him a double motive.

If she told Marc—he might have some ideas—the records . . . but he would be furious, presented with a fantasy he could not then refuse to disprove: the twenty-year-old-trail he had laughed at and which would certainly exasperate Jouvet. François? François would listen, she knew, but would detest every word of it—a tangled web of legalities in the last days of his holiday, when he had just started to sleep like a baby. And after all, might it not still be Gilbert in spite of everything! Surely at least she must first check one cross-reference . . .

She drove home slowly, parked carefully at the villa. It was when you were disturbed and preoccupied that accidents happened, and an accident might be very convenient to someone. But as she walked up the front steps François called to her from the door. "Come quickly, Laura, Solange is on the phone and she says Franchot is talking!"

She ran, she flew; never had she seen François look quite so young or so silly as when he handed her the phone and retreated, grinning, to the salon. "Well, I have been working on him," came Solange's practical voice, "every day. You are French, I said, and French you shall talk, for all you think your own language is better; o will do for water, but not for bread! And to François he has just said, *'Papa, viens tôt!'* "

"Truly?" She listened, breath suspended, as Solange gave the receiver to Franchot. "Franchot?" There was a silence on the line, a considering silence, and considerable heavy breathing: no minor task, this, for a one year old! "Franchot, speak to me!" Pause; and then the voice came. *"Maman!"* He was half-turned to Solange, not to the mouthpiece. *"Maman! C'est Maman!"* And a chuckle, a crow of triumph and astonishment at his own marvelous cleverness—the most delightful sound in the whole world.

After which it was agony to ask for Robert, to touch once again on that dark pit of corruption and say, "Robert, do you remember when your father saw Edith Lemay for the last time and quoted Phèdre at you? What did he say?"

"Exactly? Ah, mon Dieu! What a question! But . . . mon Dieu, yes, wait a moment . . . how does it go? 'Mais non, grands Dieux!' and what follows?"

" *'Qu'en un profond oubli . . .'* " said Laura slowly.

" *'Cet horrible secret demeure enseveli.'* Very good, Laura. And this horrible secret, you have unburied it?" He was amused, but she was not.

"Perhaps, Robert, thank you." Twice now, twice unmistakably, the voice of Edith Lemay had spoken to her—and as she turned, Jeanne Calvet was at her elbow, walking racket in hand to the door. Was it meant? "Madame," she said hurriedly, "may I speak to you a moment somewhere?"

"I am just going to play tennis with my husband—then we go to supper . . . can it . . ."

"Then this evening sometime? It is about your—about this affair at the villa. Will you . . . ?"

"This evening I play tennis again—with the pro," and she grinned or grimaced: her perennial tennis had, after all, brought her Gilbert. "But afterward . . . I should be through by nine . . . at the courts? They are not hard to find and very quiet at that hour!"

"That is early for him to talk!" exclaimed Marie-Gisèle, impressed and not entirely pleased with the news François had pressed upon her the moment she walked in the door carrying a dress box under her arm. "Marco and André—neither said much until they were two! You should be very proud of him!"

"Ah well," said Marc, emerging too from the salon, "if you have a lawyer for a father . . ."

"But you have bought something! Let me see." Laura's eyes were, now, for the essential. "See—and admire too, I hope!" So, the men looking tolerantly after them, they took the stairs to Marie-Gisèle's bedroom. It was indeed a charming outfit, navy with white sailor collar and cuffs, and a low waistline reminiscent of the twenties. "It gives you," said Laura admiring, "the air of a lieutenant's wife who is quite certain her husband will make admiral."

"Do you think so?" She preened. "Then my instincts were right—for that is exactly how I do want to look! But it is too long by an inch or so—if you could turn it up for me, Laura—I have pins—I could hem it and wear it tonight to dinner. Would you?"

Obediently Laura knelt, tugged, and gently folded. "And" —Marie-Gisèle—"we shall make a night of it, shall we? After all, only one more full day left!"

Laura hesitated and took the pins from her mouth. Set against laughter from Franchot, her earlier suspicions seemed fantastic, unreal. But after all . . . Did she trust Marie-Gisèle? Yes, she did; somehow in the last two weeks intimacy had flowered, delicate but secure. "Yes—only I have to meet Mme. Calvet at nine at the tennis courts, so perhaps . . ."

Marie-Gisèle pricked up her ears, looked down at the top of Laura's head. "Are you detecting again?"

"No!—Well, perhaps a little. I looked up Mme. Lemay's former producer today in Saintes—imagine, he was the man in the white suit we saw last night in the restaurant. And talking to him left me with one question she may be able to clear up . . . So would you . . . just remember where I am going?"

Marie-Gisèle nodded solemnly. "And you don't want Marc to know, right? Very good. I shall say we will take a walk on the beach while they go to their little bar—trust me, I can arrange it!"

And she did—but she looked after Laura a little forlornly, a little hesitant, as she swung inland toward the courts and the trees around it . . . August, and it was getting dark; but Jeanne Calvet spotted Laura readily and came toward her, racket swinging. *"Et voilà!* He has just left, my pro, and we had a good game. Look, just inside the trees there is a bench, if you want to . . ." They sat down. "Was it something about those men you wanted to ask me?"

"No." Half a day and Laura was still quite unprepared, no clever approach ready . . . "I just wanted to ask one thing: did you know that she was your grandmother?"

So simple to say no, you must be mad, to say "I don't know what you are talking about"—but like fine china shattered, Jeanne Calvet's face cracked into a million pieces, became the face of a very old woman, except for its tiny chin and sharp teeth the face of Edith Lemay.

"Of course it is not important"—somehow in the moment of this collapse compassion seemed imperative—"and you can, if you like, deny it. But the birth records . . . I only wondered, you see, because you said nothing, it did not seem to affect you . . ."

The face took on a younger shape, beauty returned: the face of the Girl in the Black Velvet Hat, tough, energetic, willful. Jeanne Calvet turned it to her squarely. "Well then— I knew, of course, afterward. But though you may think the worse of me for it, I was not sorry; there was no meaning . . . She came to see me when I was small, perhaps once a year, but she never liked me. Children can tell, you know—in fact sometimes I've thought she actively hated me—for my mother's death, perhaps? And after I was twelve she never came again. So what was I to do? Go about weeping and crying, 'My poor grandmother.' Involve Jean in a nasty murder case. It was bad enough, as it turned out, that I knew Machicoulet! In fact for days I have been terrified. I thought she had mentioned me in her will perhaps, left some note about me—but thank God there was nothing, not even a syllable. So I kept quiet . . . as I hope—oh, how I hope"—she put a hand on Laura's knee, beseechingly—"that you will too!"

Laura clasped the hand, in compunction. Oh, the grief, the terror! It was all simple now, the pattern of error, the cycle of destruction! Edith Lemay's illegitimate child, raised by her sister, going to work or to holiday in Poitiers . . . that child's child of shame set yet further from her grandmother, raised in Poitiers perhaps because Robert's father had funds to administer for her, perhaps—she hoped not—for a darker reason . . . But did this child, clasping her hand so anxiously, know the pattern? Need she know, if she did not? What good could possibly come of it? She temporized. "It was the sight of you, I suppose, that gave her the shock there by the villa?"

Jeanne Calvet shrugged sadly. "I suppose . . . As for me, I did not even see her! Say that you will say nothing, that Jean need not know . . ."

Again, as always, her first anxiety was for her husband. Love—or fear? "Does he know, your husband?"

"No. No!" Her cry was emphatic. "I never told him. That I am born out of wedlock, *that* I am sure he guesses, and it has never made any difference to him. But whose child, no, please, that you will not make public? The gossip, the scandal —and the moment is now so critical . . ."

Laura let out her breath. Was it, after all, just possible that they were both innocent? This one, almost certainly, was; the sight of Jacques Leclerc from her window which had given him an alibi also came close to giving her one; very near the critical time she had been curled up in her bedroom reading. Had one the right—ah, could one possibly summon up the inhumanity!—to tell this girl she had married her uncle? And yet—and yet—was it possible that the careful Jean Calvet, who had so meticulously learned his father's business, had not at some time—though perhaps not until a political career came into question—not made it his affair to learn his wife's antecedents? And then—what an appallingly powerful motive! For it was not at the time of their marriage—in her seclusion she had not even heard of that—but at the time of this child's birth that Edith Lemay had uttered those two ominous, those two dreadful lines of Racine about family incest. What had the gentle-hearted Hippolytus said, sparing his father? "Phèdre had a mother, a family, my lord, richer in all these horrors than was mine . . ." But Theseus had not listened, had not investigated in depth, and so the innocent Hippolytus had died. Just so, though not quite so innocent, might Gilbert Machicoulet one day die at the hands of the law . . .

Jeanne Calvet saw that the matter hung in the balance and added more weight to the scales. "My husband is not an ordinary man." Her chin went up proudly, and Laura remembered Calvet's praise of Mme. de Montespan: "brilliant, lovely, an entirely fitting consort for a king . . ." "He will, almost surely, one day be President of France. Oh yes, and he will be a good one, I promise you! But whatever is in the future, madame, I can assure you that your silence, and your husband's—have you told him?"

Laura shook her head, unthinking. "No, no one."

"Well then, so much the simpler! I told Jean I was coming to meet you tonight; he was worried. When I go back I can not, of course, say what we talked about, but if he knows I have reason to be grateful to you . . . There is no end, you know, to the benefits my husband's influence might bring to a lawyer." And she nodded briskly, in tacit complicity.

And somehow the scales swayed, in a wind from beyond the grave, a breath of Edith Lemay's self-will swept away by a strong wind of repentance . . . Laura sat up. "I cannot say —not yet. Mme. Calvet, I must have time to think it over— and to discuss it, perhaps, with one other person." Marc— Marc could sort implication from evidence, could by his own private investigative sources decide whether it was worthwhile to proceed with this. "But I promise you that if it is at all possible, no one else in the world shall know."

It was not good enough. Jeanne Calvet rose, with a faint hiss of displeasure, knuckles whitening upon her racket. "No, madame—for me even one other person is too many. Consider—consider again—until tomorrow! I had thought that you would understand my situation—know what I would suffer if my husband came to harm through me! Even now I feel that you . . . But if in the end it appears that I misjudged you—think then what *harm* Jean Calvet can do to François LeBreton!"

And, with a last significant nod, she turned on her heel and marched away, the tilt of her arrogant head, the firm swing of her hips, an echo of her grandmother. Watching her go, Laura exhaled a deep and broken sigh. Neither her last appeal nor her threat had been made in vain. She was indeed sorry for Jeanne Calvet, twice Calvet and once Lemay: afraid for her marriage, her husband, afraid perhaps even *of* her husband. And her enmity, like his, would be implacable; even where he now stood upon the ladder Jean Calvet could injure François in many subtle and bitter ways. Marc was even more vulnerable; for all the vaunted independence of the PJ everyone knew there were strings to be pulled: was Marie-Gisèle not perfectly right after all in thinking they might be pulled both ways? And even to say to Marc, "I think this," would be quite possibly to destroy his career—for Marc was an honorable man, and he would ask questions, and the questions would drift back to listening ears . . . Was it to be she, Laura, who would dash all the hopes of Marie-Gisèle in her sailor suit? No, no, bury it again in the grave!

And yet it would not stay buried. She knew clearly that, not brought to light, it would haunt her to her dying days. She would live inextricably tied to that corruption. It would not stay buried perhaps even to external reality. Jean and Jeanne Calvet had no children—by whose choice? And supposing that choice were to be reversed, or that accident—what Minotaur? She groaned aloud; what was her moral responsibility? Involuntarily bowing her head, she prayed "Oh God . . ."

And, by that second's impulse of prayer, the blow landed where it was not intended, well behind her ear, not at the temple. Yet it was vicious, powerful, and she fell forward, hands clutching grass, the first fallen leaves. Fingers scrabbled; she must get up, must somehow avert what . . . But a heavy weight dropped on her back; hands, tough and supple, captured her throat, pressed intolerably; no lifting, no purchase . . . Her head pounded, blackness deeper than twilight enveloped her; only as, hands wide, clutching, she plunged into it she thought she heard a voice calling, "Laura!" and made one last effort to answer it . . .

Vainly.

CHAPTER 22

When her eyes opened, it was to an uncomfortable place. Hard for lying, sharp and bright to the pupils, unbearably loud to the ear. Loud voices, a blur of a face . . . She squinted; it just might be François. She turned her head slightly, toward the voices, and the pain was intolerable . . . but that was Marc, surely, at her other side and beyond him a great deal of white, white people, white walls, white lights . . . She shut her eyes against them and groped for meaning . . . of course, a hospital. She was dying, they were all at her bedside . . . The tears brimmed in her eyes, total despair and self-pity . . . dying so young, and her poor Franchot motherless . . . but François was saying, "She opened her eyes! Laura! Laura!"

She wished he would not shout so loudly; surely, if one were dying, people ought to be quiet! She struggled with pain, wanting only to crawl back into the darkness, but a hand took hers, gently, warm; there, that was better! Some current that evened the agony in her head; that, if she did not move, did not break its flow, would make living almost tolerable . . . "Laura, you went to the tennis courts. To meet Mme. Calvet. What happened?"

Yes, it was true. But what had happened? There was no recollection. And Marc's voice was harsher even than François's, quite unbearable . . . "I'm dying," she said reproachfully at them.

"No, you are not." François's tone now was quiet, caressing. "Not to say that if you did not have a hard head . . . Marie saved your life, you know. She followed you, and when

Mme. Calvet left and you did not come, she went to find you
. . . Who was it struck you?"

Yes, what he said was true, and "Not her." She could remember that. "I saw her go. It was after . . ."

Even with eyes closed, she could feel them nodding to one
another, beaming encouragingly. "Then what was it you
knew that you did not tell us?" Marie said. "It must have
been important, you know—one does not get hit on the head
for nothing!" This was Marc, and "hit on the head" pierced
her like an awl. She stirred, resentfully, and it was agony.

"Tell us, love." It was barely a whisper. "We must know,
you see, to keep you safe—even here . . ."

"It was silly." In so much pain, how could one make the
effort—speculations, addled in addled brainpan. "Silly or not,
tell us. In five words, if you can manage that, but tell us."

The current was stronger, tender and tranquil; perhaps
she was in fact not dying. But why did her throat hurt, rasp-
ing? In five words? Impossible. Fifteen? Could she just manage? "Jean Calvet married his niece—but I think—he may
also have married his daughter." Silence, incredulous, something still lacking. Three more words. "Edith Lemay's grand-
daughter." And if they were too stupid to put that together,
so much the worse for them . . .

In the room absolute silence. Furiously calculating silence,
perhaps, but it set up no counterrhythm to the pain, and she
could listen to the throbbing, go with it, drift . . .

A door banged, and she cried out involuntarily, opened her
eyes. A hurried bulk filled the room, crowded the pain.
"There *was* something in the wound—and the doctor kept
it!" Jouvet's voice was rich with satisfaction. "Plastic again?"
"No—wood. The same weapon, but this time it is marked!
The men are searching the park . . ." "Not the park, the
villa." Marc was incisive. Another voice, this time at her head
—and she had not even seen its owner—furiously angry but
thank God whispering. "Now that is enough—my patient
. . . !" A woman; how nice! and one with some sense of how
people who hurt should be treated . . . More whispers, ur-

gent and sibilant, and then grateful silence, only François's hand still in hers.

Much later, she was awake again. He did not seem to have moved. "François?" "Yes." He must be getting stiff. "Move a little!"

Obediently, he shifted. "Did I make sense, earlier?"

"Oh yes, I think so." He was considering. "But Laura"—and there was a hint of pain in it—"why didn't you tell me?"

She was still in too much pain to work out a lie. "I thought you would not believe me."

The suffering in his voice deepened. "But why? Why would I not believe you?"

It opened, the truth in herself, deeper and deeper. "I make so many mistakes—Paul, Harry . . ."

There was an even longer silence. "Am I a mistake, then, too?"

It was not at *all* what she had meant. "No, not you! Me . . . It was so fantastic . . . and I know my judgment is bad. Not yours . . . I love you, François." And the current in the hands flowed both ways. *"My* fault."

Now the quality of the silence had changed: it was peaceful, considering. "But I do not know why you should think that, Laura. Harry respected your judgment—married you, it seems to me, because you *were* dependable. Paul certainly respected you or he would not have tried to kill you. As for your judgment—you are alive and rich, aren't you? And you cannot always at first," he folded his fingers over hers comfortably, "find a paragon like me!"

She found that, aching head or no, she was smiling. Warmth, joy, that he was at last speaking casually, sensibly, of Harry and Paul whom he never mentioned; speaking what, after all, must be the truth or he would not say it. There were advantages, after all, in . . . "I am going to live, aren't I?"

"Oh yes—this time." His tone was faintly grim. "But next time, Laura—tell me?"

"I will." Of course. They were indeed two separate people,

but in matters which counted, there would always only be one of them . . . It hurt, surely, less. She snuggled a little, experimentally. Sleep—this time she would truly sleep. Only one more thing: "Did they arrest him?" He contemplated this, pondering. "Yes," he said at last, "they have made an arrest."

CHAPTER 23

It was long afterward, a gray Paris day in November with the rain drifting down, a day for meditating upon the inwardness of things, that she read the statements Sarrazin had at last smuggled off to her. The Leclercs were long gone, back in Marseille, with Yvonne fiercely clutching the emerald necklace and saying to Laura, "This he will not get his hands on, this is Jacquot's future." And the Italian family was back in Milan, dining out on their mystery with joyous gesticulations. But Michel and Germaine Moreuil were there—one summer friendship had somehow lingered on. "It is useful," François had observed with some surprise, "to know a man who knows everything, even feudal land tenure." Germaine was, these days, far more peaceful; and so was Marie-Gisèle, by the fire, knitting: one of the incidental results of their holiday was that in late April there would be a fifth Tavernier, and the larger apartment was already on lease. Marc, however, was absent, out on a case—and besides he knew it all already, had known it as soon as they found the stained tennis racket which brought a confession.

Two confessions.

"I knew, but I did not know she knew. It was after we were some five years married, and I had begun to think of politics. One never knows what one's adversaries may use against one, and her illegitimacy . . . I wanted to be forearmed. So I hired, God help me, a firm of private investigators to track down her true mother . . .

"They came to me with the records: father unknown, they said. Ah, but I knew . . . I knew . . ." The *greffier's* notes here observed that for a time the suspect had been unable to continue.

"Well, what was I to do? I loved her . . . I met her first at a nightclub I frequented, she was only a waitress—but so alive, so forthright, so intelligent! I started to see her—it was perfectly aboveboard, at first I felt, God help me, no more than paternal . . . An uncle, perhaps," the word underlined in immense despair and irony . . . "who wanted to find more suitable work for her. She was obviously too good for that environment. Then, gradually . . .

"I had never loved another woman, you know. Only her mother. I was twenty-one that summer, she was nineteen, working at the *mercerie*, and we swore nothing would ever come between us, not parents, not money . . . I was going to marry her, to ask my mother's permission; my father was dead then and he had never . . . Then the old woman came posthaste from Paris . . . She was so gentle, my love, had never harmed anyone, it was not in her. It destroyed her, knowing what she had done, unwitting. I saw her die then in front of my eyes, a flower turning brown, withered in an instant. For me, I cursed my father, her, the old woman, I was wild, furious. And for years afterward I trusted no one, no woman; they betrayed, you see; that, or one killed them not meaning to.

"Jeanne was not in the least like Lisette; yet there was something. We thought alike, fought alike. She was intensely interested in me, in all I did, in my career—she was fiercely ambitious for me! And then—one could not resist her.

"Why not I thought. Her origins—she was convent-taught, after all, quick to learn—and I am not exactly a duke, you know! She could be, unlikely as it might seem, an excellent wife for a politician . . . All these rationalizations! and it was really that—we were so much alike, you see!"

Again, the *greffier* noted, there followed a long break in the interrogation. When it was resumed the magistrate spoke first, her voice presumably matter-of-fact and incisive. "Her," because the original *juge d'instruction* had firmly and cannily refused to believe the Calvets and his Lemay case had anything to do with one another, and a new *commission rogatoire* had been issued by the district's only woman judge to deal with "violent assault upon Laure LeBreton, visitor . . ."

"You told the police, at the time of the search of your rooms, that you had killed Mme. Lemay. Let us explore that a little. Did you know, at the time you came here, that she lived in Pontaillac?"

"No, I had no idea."

"And the afternoon of the day she was killed, when she was in front of the Villa Brise de Mer, did you see her?"

"No. I came up from the beach and straight in the door."

"The next day, did you discuss her death with your wife at all?"

"No . . . I was afraid . . . I was not sure she knew that was her grandmother."

"But you—you knew."

"Yes—And I was glad. There was always the fear, you see, that someone else would . . . Now the last person, the only person, was dead."

"And later, did you come to suspect that your wife might in fact be aware of the relationship?"

"No—no. Only"—here he had obviously hesitated—"when it emerged that she had been involved with a jewel thief . . . It was so unlike her, she was always extremely discreet. And I could not believe that . . . We never lied to each other, never!"

"Only, I gather, by silence!" Here the magistrate's tone must have been extremely dry. "There is, I believe, some question of a plastic racket cover, missing from one of your tennis rackets; as they are of the same mark, no one knows which. Can you clarify this matter for us? Was it yours? When and how did it disappear?"

"I cannot tell you."

"And the ring and pin that disappeared from Mme.

Lemay's body—can you tell us how and when it was placed in M. Machicoulet's drawer?"

"No."

"When it comes to matters of fact, it seems you can tell us very little!"

"Madame, I have admitted there was another relationship between my wife and me, on Commissaire Jouvet's assurance that if a confession were made, this fact would not be made public at the trial. As for the rest—when my wife makes her statement, I will agree to whatever is in it."

François roused. "I thought, at first, that his lawyer had talked some sense into him during the break. But not after that last sentence!"

"No." Germaine Moreuil spoke with unexpected gentleness. "That, I think, was chivalry."

Marie-Gisèle looked at her knitting as if she had never seen it before. "I always wondered why they had no children. Types like that, they usually want to carry on their sacred image . . . He did confess, then."

"Yes—just after they found the racket, with my blood still on it!" Laura was a little indignant still. "In the hall closet at the villa—but of course everyone knew who belonged to it. There was no way, then, that they could . . ."

"And she?"

"Jouvet said she was frightened a moment, but only a moment. She played fair, that one—like her grandmother." She picked up the second sheaf of paper in her lap. "It is curious, you know—the same qualities, the same defects . . . She tells it just as it was, no regrets, no excuses—she had to save him, after all." And she began to read.

"I killed her, of course. When she took that turn, in front of the villa, I knew she had recognized me. And Jean, of course. I thought there was a good chance she would not tell, and I thought about that all the rest of the day. In the evening Jean was out, and I went to play tennis as usual, with whom I don't know: some kid who considered himself a hotshot. But I had found out where her house was: it was on my way home. I thought I would plead with her, reason, but the moment she opened the door I could see—the look she gave me! She always hated me.

"The racket was still in my hand, in its case, and I did not think at all. As she turned, I swung, sidewise, from the doorstep, and she dropped, like that . . . I stepped inside, closed the door, and kept hitting until I was sure she was dead. In that narrow space it was difficult, but I have a good forehand.

"It was only just dark, but no one was on the street, no sound from the neighbors. I thought, but that is not enough, she may have an old name and address, a letter, even her will . . . I went upstairs, stepping over her carefully, put on a pair of her white gloves, searched the house and took whatever I thought might . . . I was careful, thorough; it was important. When I came to her will I thought I should take it too and then I remembered, if there were none they might have to trace heirs. So I read it, saw it was harmless, tied it again and left it.

"When I was sure nothing was left there, I had only to step out. But then, in the hall, I thought it should look like a robbery, and I bent and took her ring and her pin. I did not realize how troublesome they would be to get rid of.

"I waited at the hedge till I saw no one was coming, walked out with my racket, went down to the sea. I took the cover and threw it as far as I could. Even if it washed up, who would look twice? I buried the address book and the letters under a rock, below the tide line; they would soon be unreadable. I should have thrown the ring and pin away too, but if they were ever found that would destroy the picture I had built up.

"But then, unfortunately, it did not quite come out as I had planned. They would look for thieves, it seemed to me, and not find them: there was no connection between us at all. Who would have thought that, at the same villa, there would be four other people who knew her? So the police came, and the lawyer's wife told me they suspected M. Leclerc. I could not have that—he was my cousin, after all! I thought quickly,

and gave him an alibi—I did not want to put myself in the
police eye at all, but I was sure she would tell them. And—
that was clever, I think, on such short notice—I added the
one little detail that would be convincing, the balding spot on
the top of his head; I had noticed it passing him one day in the
dining room.

"Afterward, I realized I had given myself a kind of alibi too;
but still they did not go away, and I was getting tired of it—I
wanted it finished. I had already made the acquaintance of
M. Machicoulet and his friend—I had some idea what sort of
men they were. They would not be missed, I thought. I let
him make some advances, told him I would come to his room
at ten-thirty, to leave his door open when he went out. Instead I came earlier, left my ring and my grandmother's
jewelry, and when he came—I made sure he had no suspicions. But when my husband came home I found I was very
distraught—it is true, I was!—I was lying to him, and I had
never lied to him, never! Only some things I had not said.
And it was, after all, for his career I was lying, for which I had
done everything that I did!

"Well then—you know the rest. I had done the right thing
—as it turned out, they deserved what was coming to them,
every bit of it. Only somehow she found out, Mme. LeBreton,
I still cannot think how! And suddenly it became far too
complicated. I could not let her say what she knew, there was
no help for it. It was very hard—in a way I had liked her very
much, but I thought of my husband, I circled back, and I
acted. If I had had time . . . but I did not, and she did not
die and the police came and there was blood on the racket
and I could not let them arrest Jean. *Et voilà*, I have confessed, she was my grandmother, I hated her, and I killed her.
That is all you need to know, and all I will testify to."

There was a silence. "And in the end she testified to nothing at all." François. Laura shivered. "To slit your wrist with a
pin hidden in your skirt hem—have you any idea how long
that must have taken, in her cell? And the courage? And, in a
sense, I killed her—Now," and she looked at François di-

rectly, "now we have both killed someone." Yet it was not a weight of guilt, but a fact, a shared understanding—in a way—

"In a way," said Marie-Gisèle, "we all kill someone, a little, every day. How do I know what I am raising my boys to? What kind of love, misguided, that will someday destroy them, or some other person? Do you remember, François, that day at La Rochelle when you told us, 'The sins of the fathers are visited upon the children, even to the fourth generation?' "

"He said that?" Michel Moreuil was intrigued.

"Certainly it was true." Germaine was categoric, as usual. "She was exactly like her grandmother—the energy, the self-will, even the courage." And it was notable that she spoke of Edith Lemay as if she were just another human being, no better, no worse than the rest of us. Notable, too, that Michel responded in exactly the same way. *Mais enfin,* it is interesting, that. Why the *fourth* generation? Why not the third, or fifth? Had they some sense that after eighty years, the genetic inheritance had been bred out, watered down?"

"The fourth generation—I suppose that's Jacquot!" Laura was amused. "And my guess is that there is now no problem there . . . So that is the moral of it all—four generations, and the old sins can be forgotten?"

"No," said Marie-Gisèle decisively, folding her knitting and dipping her head toward Laura. "The moral is that a good classical education is never wasted. Even Jouvet, Marc tells me, is now determined his boys will spend their time at the lycée more seriously!"

They all looked at her, lost, and she looked back at them in astonishment. "Well, think a little! Who is the real unraveler of our mystery? Where would we all be, without Jean Racine and *Phèdre?*"

Amy Marsland has published several works of nonfiction and her short stories have appeared in many magazines. She lives in Greene, New York, where she is treasurer and former editor of a weekly newspaper chain. *A Classic Death* is her second novel for the Crime Club.